D0546452

The Place

Nancy Osa

ISBN 979-8-9876174-0-3
eISBN 979-8-9876174-1-0
Library of Congress Catalog Card Number: 0000-0000

Copyright 2023 NHPC with Original Story by Nancy Osa
https://theplace.newhopeproductsco.com

Printed in the United States of America

All rights reserved. No part of this book shall be reproduced or transmitted in any form or by any means, electronic, mechanical, magnetic, photographic including photocopying, recording or by any information storage and retrieval system, without prior written permission of the publisher. No patent liability is assumed with respect to the use of the information contained herein. Although every precaution has been taken in the preparation of this book, the publisher and author assume no responsibility for errors or omissions. Neither is any liability assumed for damages resulting from the use of the information contained herein.

This is a work of fiction. Names, characters, places, and incidents either are the product of the author's imagination or are used fictitiously. Any resemblance to actual events or locales or persons, living or dead , is entirely coincidental.

Published February 2023

For the next generation

The author wishes to thank: Joe Shumaker for his inspiration and public service; Mary Shumaker and Patricia Burke for their thoughtful suggestions; and Ken Morris for his invaluable first-reader support and, especially, for channeling the voice of Kavi.

DRAMATIS PERSONAE.

WOMEN.

CARLITA HALL, our heroine
BRISA FLORES, her best friend

MEN.

CHRIS HAMADA, their high school classmate
DEAN DIXON, a jock
KAVI DAS, a community college student

SECONDARY.

JOSS MORALES, stage play director
DAVID BOLNES, student actor
MALIA KENDRAKE, student actor
MASON JONES, student actor
BLAZE HEYDEN, student actor

"THE DIRECTORS," Jack and Loretta

Chapter 1

The BS started flying before the last audition was over. And if you think snark, lies, and conspiracy theories are unique to politicians and basement bloggers, you should hear theater people. Masters of the bullshit universe.

"We are nothing if not creative..." I murmured, frowning at my phone.

The theater chat feed was thick with speculation and little actual news. The budget for the play was either the biggest or the crappiest ever. Rehearsals wouldn't leave time for dinner or would be catered, with free booze, but only for the stars. The director had already picked the main cast. No high schooler had a chance. *Then why have us try out?* I wondered. All of that stuff could not be true at the same time.

And yet, I had to know. This was the second-most crucial thing I had ever wanted: a shot at the lead role in what had to be the sickest reboot of a period piece since *Hamilton*. It would go a long way toward making up for not getting the first-most crucial thing I had ever wanted. But waiting to find out might kill me.

I sighed. How long could I hold out? Dubiously, I hit Brisa's number in my contacts. My best friend was always a font of information, which could either be 100 percent trustworthy or completely made up. It was a crap shoot, but if B. didn't have answers, at least she and I could not-know together.

We never bothered with greetings. "Can you believe Joss wants rehearsals on Friday nights!" The outrage in Brisa's voice was at 7 on a scale that I had developed over the years based on tone, intensity, and decibel level. The fifth of six kids in the Flores family, Brisa carried a sense of injustice everywhere she went. Someone else always had the stuff or the satisfaction that she wanted.

"She's your cousin," I pointed out. "Can't you get her to change it?"

Brisa's pout triangulated off the cell towers. "*La vaca* has the last word. You don't mess with the director."

"Look. What good are family ties if you can't exploit them?"

Brisa chuckled. "I already did. Don't tell anyone, but Joss already promised me AD."

I smiled to myself. It was all falling into place. With Brisa as assistant director, the intel would flow our way. "Did she give you any idea who's getting Kate?" Kate Hardcastle was the play's young female lead, the one who would have the most memorable lines and the sexiest costumes, opposite whoever was chosen to play the conflicted young stud—probably some college guy, hopefully not too full of himself. There were just as many drama kings as queens out there.

"Hell no. She's announcing the cast tomorrow. In person. On campus. We all have to be there."

"So she can see the shame in our eyes when we don't make the cut," I supposed. I still felt as though I had nailed my reading, but the chatter online had opened a chasm of doom beneath my tower of optimism.

"No, so she can enlist the losers in doing the grunt work," Brisa corrected me. "Joss knows once they're there, it won't be easy to wriggle out of backstage assignments."

Smart. Crap. *"Mañana,* then," I said, resigned.

"But, hey," Brisa put in. "This might be our last Friday night as free women. Let's go bother the guys."

A worthy pastime. "You got it," I agreed. "See you at the place."

***

There were only two main ways in and out of the new home I shared with Mom in the wooded trailer park: a road off the highway, and a network of hiking trails that connected to a local through-way, one of those bike-and-hike paths developed by the county on an old railway bed. The city park that the path intersected closed its gates at dusk, but the miles-long ribbon of pavement couldn't be shut down. A viaduct supporting a pedestrian overpass formed a natural shelter that Foster High kids had claimed as a hangout spot. This was my saving grace—I could get out of "the community" without having to beg a ride or take the bus.

I grabbed a headlamp, even though the days were getting longer, and hit the loop trail at the end of our street. This spoked off through the trees and ferns to a rougher path that linked to the paved county corridor about a half-mile away. Then it was just a short jog to the place. We had never given it any other name; the spot hosted a rotating guest list of anyone who showed up on any given day or night. Fridays, though, guaranteed the most company.

A smattering of fists raised for bumps as I ducked under the overpass. There were a few people from Spanish class whose accents were better than mine, a guy who always sat in the same seat at lunch with two of his friends, and the usual knot of Pioneers jocks whose voices were the loudest and who acknowledged anyone outside their group by making public comments about them that discouraged any polite conversation. One of them, a tall, basketball or baseball kind of guy, had been at play try-outs. I remembered him because it was odd for one of his crowd to color outside the lines.

"Hey," came a soft, male voice, along with a proffered fist, which I tapped as I passed by.

"Zup," I said, noting once more in the fading light that my neighbor's eyelashes were longer than any

I'd ever seen, on a male or female. With his head of fine, black hair, delicate facial structure, and those luxurious eyelashes, Chris Hamada was arguably more beautiful than either of his two sisters. He drew gazes from men and women, and was probably a shoo-in for a major role onstage. He'd nabbed two leads at Foster High before, once, improbably, as the devil in *Damn Yankees.* He and I had met on the bus to school from Worden's Woods, along with the small population of community residents who were past their toddler years and under the age of fifty-five.

"Hey, Carls!" Brisa waved me over to our favorite corner of concrete abutment, and Chris fell in beside me.

"If it isn't Carlotta Hall Monitor," one of the jocks announced as I passed by.

"It's *Carlita, cochon,*" Brisa retorted, sticking up for me, and we high-fived as the *pig* epithet sailed over the guy's head. Spanish was the verbal currency in the Flores household, unlike in mine. If I had to bank on my command of the language, I wouldn't be able to break a five. Hence the need for Spanish 310.

Brisa smiled at Chris. "Hamad, heard you were good today at try-outs."

He dipped his head in false humility and said, "Where'd you hear that?"

"Oh, here and there."

I nodded, knowing that Brisa might blab, but she'd never give away her sources. To have the goods and not use them: that was power.

Brisa leaned in and exchanged eyelash flutters with Chris. "Did you know that it's gonna be an all–high school cast? Well, it's almost for sure."

"What?" he squeaked.

I pressed my lips together. "Come on. Why would Joss do that? It's a community college production."

Brisa kept a straight face. "Same reason they invite us to try out in the first place. They don't have enough theater majors. And there are already too many extracurric options for the amateurs. Who wants to work their ass off for a play when they could be doing musical bowling or dessert crawls?"

"Me," I answered without thinking, then added, "wait. What's a dessert crawl?"

Chris cut off a reply with both palms. "Who cares? The odds of us getting cast just went up astronomically." He paused. "Actually, by a factor of ... 9.4."

Now I didn't know which of the two were more shocking—Chris, with his photographic recall and ability to estimate crowd numbers and demographics—or Brisa, with her talent for complete poker-faced fabrication. "I call BS, Flores. No way did Joss say it'd be a high school–only cast. There were tons of Foothills students auditioning." I narrowed my eyes at Brisa, trying to elicit a giggle or confession.

But my friend just raised her chin and murmured, "I'm not saying if she did or she didn't."

"But you just did!"

Brisa tugged at the hennaed ends of her long, thick, black-brown hair and then tossed them over her shoulder, never admitting to a thing. She had probably spent more time on her eye makeup today than an entire lifetime's worth of contemplation of her inconsistencies. Blue-green lid shadow abruptly met inky waterproof eyeliner and mascara in a show of force, directly contrasting with personal boundaries that were more ... permeable, I mused. Quite the opposite of my own predictable, rational standards, consistently applied to all situations—unless parental consent was needed for something. Well, parents had to be set up to do the right thing.

Brisa reached out and grabbed the Coke can Chris was holding and took a swig. He totally let her, so she gave it back without a fuss. Then he offered it to me.

I hesitated.

"Vaxxed and no symptoms," he said, reading my mind, so I took it.

Nearby, a wave of laughter rose from the athletic crowd that had grown so large it spilled out onto the paved trail. A track-and-field girl performed an exaggerated shake, letting her butt cheeks lead the rest of her body around in half circles. One voice boomed above the rest of them: "Amanda Perry climbs to the top of the charts with her hit single, 'I Want Some Maximus in My Gluteus'!"

Chris half-stifled a laugh and said admiringly, "The dancer's got some chops."

Brisa put in, "And the DJ's not so bad himself, with that honey voice and ... honey everything else. Dean Dixon. Doesn't he do that Tuesday-Thursday lunchtime radio show at school?"

It was the jock who had come to try-outs. Tall, handsome, *and* a seductive broadcaster's voice. "I hate him," I said, and my friends popped eyeballs at me. "I mean, the show's great. But a guy who has it all and everything comes easy to him?" I just shook my head, never mind that, not so long ago, that could have been said about me. *Not my type,* I thought stubbornly.

Chris was still watching Dean cut up for his audience. "Oh, I don't know. Maybe just the luck of the draw. Maybe it's not all roses for the guy."

"Maybe he cuts wicked farts and can't help it," Brisa suggested, also keeping her eyes on his athletic build. Tall enough for basketball, lithe enough to pitch a baseball game, Dean Dixon was the picture of potential. His knee-length, red shorts showed tight calves that flexed and popped as he shifted his weight, and the sleeves of his gray knit shirt were pushed up to emphasize his softball-sized biceps. I would only confess to myself that the aesthetics were top-notch, farts or no farts.

Our talk turned to more speculation about the play, then an outdoor concert that was coming up, and whether there would be a senior skip day this year after every senior got Saturday detention last year. Since we all were juniors, the prospect of the whole senior class being jailed for a day was both not applicable to us and delicious.

After a while, people started to pick up their bikes or drift off to parked cars. We three friends lingered, not wanting to leave, until one of the sporting crowd shouldered into Chris, pretending he hadn't noticed him. "Sorry, ladies," he said.

"It's *dude,* dude," Chris retorted, his pale face coloring wildly. B. and I glared daggers at the offender, then said our goodbyes to each other.

"Coming with?" I asked Chris, nodding in the direction of home.

"Sure," he said in a voice a half-octave lower than normal.

It must be tough to be a beautiful man, I thought.

***

Somehow, tomorrow came. I took some care in dressing, knowing I might be meeting my costar for the first time. A dark-olive shirt set off my green eyes, while my favorite jeans, I thought, added some substance to too-narrow hips and too-skinny legs. I added a little cheek color, but that was it for makeup, and I chose the feather earrings that other women always noticed, to break up the solid colors of my top and pants. After my shower, I had added some curl product to my shoulder-length, brown hair, which I now checked in the mirror in my room. The still-wet curls formed stripey highlights against the drying strands. Perfect.

"I hope you can handle all this, Mr. Wonderful," I addressed my potential castmate. One thing I did know: the conflicted young stud in the script— "Spider" Marlow, who woos Kate—would not be played by my neighbor. Chris had tried out for the larger but less glamorous role of Tony Lumpkin because it had greater comic opportunities. No, this was to be a blind date, assuming I got the role I felt I was destined to play.

The student-written script, *Mistakes of a Night,* was a take-off on a melodrama written in 1773, moving that British comedy of manners to present-day America but preserving much of the original, to great effect. The director/playwright had thrust colonial-era problems into today's world to show just how alike they still were. Some things never changed, I thought, and romance and money were at the top of that list. I had been surprised to see how readable and relatable the doctored script was. It was going to be so much fun. And *fun* was my watchword—ever since the pandemic had crested, and since my family had been dissected in a decidedly un-fun manner.

I looked for Chris at the bus stop, but he didn't show. Twenty-five minutes later, the bus dumped me at the edge of the Foothills Community College parking lot. I kicked aside clusters of plastic bottles and candy wrappers to join the intermittent stream of students heading inside one of the buildings. Then I made the long trek kitty-corner to the theater and art center. It was segregated like a poor stepchild from the more serious departments and offices, as though they didn't want all that frivolous thespian energy to seduce the math majors. The joke was on them, I thought, spying my neighbor out in the hall in front of the double doors. Chris was both a math guy and a comedic actor with great timing. Maybe an actor needed more math than I'd imagined.

I saw him now, and he waved limply at me, pointing at the doors to indicate they were still locked. A few other people we didn't know milled about, waiting for the same thing we were waiting for. Then a trio of honchos strode toward us.

Brisa's cousin Joss swung a lanyard of keys, and the crowd parted so she could unlock the entrance to the theater. Behind her followed Brisa, with a sheaf of papers, and a college guy I didn't know, whose fluid gait hinted at years of dance lessons. His strawberry-blond hair, translucent skin, and lanky build were quite the contrast to the two Latinas; Joss and Brisa both rocked the lower end of the color scale and the higher end of any bell curve.

Chris sidled up to me, and we drifted in through the doors with the motley assortment of Foster High kids and community college theater types. Someone snapped on the rest of the house lights. An aura of expectation surrounded the sea of a couple hundred empty seats, as well as the hopes and dreams of all of us would-be cast members, who Joss motioned up to the front rows. She ascended the black stairs and plopped down on the edge of the stage, while the rest of us took seats or milled around beneath the footlights by school groups—FCCers stage left, Pioneers stage right.

My stomach did that inverted, empty thing it did when I forgot to breathe properly for a long time. I shot a sideways look at Chris. He appeared unperturbed and excited, not desperate and ... clenchy, like me. I glanced around more widely, pretending to search for someone I knew but really taking inventory of possible challengers and costars. Why was it so easy to tell the difference between my classmates and the college students? There wasn't that much of an age gap, after all. No, it was more a sense of place. *They belong here,* I thought. *We're just visiting.*

The appeal had gone out to Foster High English and Speech classes to come try out for the play because the college department's numbers were down, not having rebounded yet after the return to in-person classes and extracurriculars. But maybe the rumor mill was right, and we'd been invited just to fill the need for set painters and ticket takers. I studied Chris's expectant face once more. He wasn't going to like that.

Strawberry must have picked up on the pessimism. He cleared his throat and struck a pose at Joss's feet, then enunciated, "Friends, Romans ... lowly high schoolers! The moment we've all been waiting for has arrived. Our supreme ruler, writer, and director, Joss Morales, is about to decree who will be the heroes of our little drama ... and who will be its beasts of burden." The snickers came from the stage-left crowd. The rest of us held our breath.

Joss waved an arm at him. "Dave B., everybody. Likes to distill things to their atomic makeup, but that's not exactly how things work around here. Yes, I am this production's supreme ruler." She grinned. "But, no, we are not otherwise hierarchical; we are a *team*. Without every single player, the show cannot go on. That means onstage and off. You are all here because we need each other, but more important:

our future audience needs you. You will be working for them—not for me, or for Dave here, or for yourselves."

My abdominal muscles relaxed ever so slightly.

Brisa spoke up. "What about for me? They will work for me, right?" she asked with mock arrogance, while really wanting that to be true.

Joss socked her in the shoulder. *"Sí, jefe.* I forgot. They do have to answer to you." She addressed the group again. "My cousin Brisa, *amigos.* She will be my assistant, meaning she will do everything I don't want to do and everything that keeps you all pulling together, to pull off—" Her voice rose. *"—the greatest show this world has ever seen!"*

The crowd buzzed, liking the prediction.

She raised her hands for quiet. "Now. To set the tone, here's what I'm going for. We take a 250-year-old script, give it a makeover to today, and transport the audience to a place they have never imagined in their wildest dreams. We confound their intellect. We make them laugh. We take their emotions to new heights, creating a sense of *yearning,* and then we satisfy that yearning."

"In short," Dave B. broke in, "we turn a British comedy of manners into a Greek tragedy."

Joss nodded. "Only with a purely American flavor. We come at it from the roots. We sing the blues."

My mind scrambled to catch up. I was still stuck back on *yearning*. To think you could use that for something—something noble, something that only art could generate.

"Okay, let's give this announcement the drama it deserves." Joss got to her feet and turned toward the stage wing. "Kavi? Some mood sound and lighting, yeah?"

Moments later, the house lights dimmed and a blue spot found the director at her mark. Synthesizer tones came through the hidden speakers, starting with a low hum and building to a crescendo. Brisa came forward and handed her papers to Joss, who waved at the wings. The music dropped to background level.

"And now, the big reveal: a role for each of you who took the time to come out, try out, or volunteer to get this production off the ground. Please join me onstage when you hear your name. From Oliver Goldsmith's *She Stoops to Conquer* to Josefina Morales's *Mistakes of a Night* ... I give you our cast and crew!" Joss pushed her short, choppy, dark hair out of her eyes and checked her roster, then began to read. "Servants..."

She rattled off several names, one a classmate of mine from last year's math class and the rest unfamiliar. I caught Chris's eye in the dim light as the suspense grew.

"Kavi?" Joss raised both palms and gave him a two-arm wave. The spot changed to three colors of flashing lights, and the music swelled once more, with a recorded drum roll added. When it subsided, the director read off the main cast: "Tony Lumpkin, played by Chris Hamada...."

I gripped Chris's arm as he jumped out of his seat. "Way to go!" I said through the applause.

"Miss Constance Neville to be played by—" a college girl who squealed and headed for the riser. "Beau Hastings will be Dave Bolnes!"

"Of course." I watched the red-headed thespian vault from the floor to the stage without even using the stairs. The guy was clearly a natural and had expected the role.

"Spider Marlow will be portrayed by—" a lithe college guy with soft-looking, longish brown hair and a massive grin. He slapped palms with his friends on the way past.

I could get used to that energy, I thought with anticipation. In the play, Spider was Kate's suitor. That meant that—

"Our next star, playing Miss Kate Hardcastle, is—"

I tensed, waiting to hear my name.

"Malia Kendrake!"

Malia...? Someone other than Carli Hall. The nervous smile froze on my face as another girl jumped up amid cheers to take her place next to the cute, long-haired guy. My stomach knifed inward, until I let out a forceful breath.

Not me. Every muscle was tight and immobile. *Brisa got in. Chris got in. But not me.*

The lights and sound fuzzed out as I tried to keep it together and not dash for the exit. "A role for each of you," Joss had said, meaning some anonymous production crew slot awaited me. B. had been right, it *was* harder to say no to the fallback position, now that I'd taken a bus across town to get here and everyone knew I didn't make the cut. Nobody wanted to be seen as a sore loser.

A hand jabbed my elbow. I shook my head and tried to hear over the pounding in my ears. "They want you," a college girl two seats over called, and I looked up to see Brisa wildly waving me forward.

"Carlita Hall? Is she here?" Joss asked impatiently.

I stumbled over the first stair and had to stick out a hand to keep from cracking my jaw on the edge of the stage. "What am I—who...?"

"Mrs. Dorothy Hardcastle, I presume," Joss said, glowing at me now, as a few kids gave me pats on the back. "Our elder stateswoman, ladies and gentlemen. Her costar, and our final cast member, will be ... as Mr. Cadbury Hardcastle, Dean Dixon!" My popular classmate bounded toward the stage amid guttural shouts from the teammates he'd brought along to witness his glory. My costar.

Oh.

The lights and sound amped up along with calls and claps for the cast, and I gave a good rendition of pleased modesty while my stomach proceeded to digest my heart. I heard Brisa's and Chris's celebratory words and Joss saying something about the first time that two high schoolers had snared the leading roles....

Wait. What?

Leading roles? The two old farts in the show? Did I *look* old? Maybe people just thought I acted old? But Dean wasn't mature in any way, and they'd cast him as the patriarch. The Hardcastles weren't even the romantic stars—those were Kate and Spider, and Constance and Beau. The cool, young characters. The sexy ones.

I turned to commiserate with Brisa but instead caught Dean Dixon looking at me with an indecipherable expression. His dark-chocolate eyes showed confusion, his parted lips emitted no sound.

Then he shook his head in a satisfied manner and pulled away to accept his friends' congratulations. He must have gotten something he wanted. But that something sure couldn't be me.

Chapter 2

What was it that made disappointment so ... disappointing? I wondered. *So I didn't get the exact role I wanted. So, what?* The instant I tried to write it off, the dissatisfaction grew exponentially. Why?

Overblown expectations could deflate a person pretty quickly. But I'd had decent odds of getting the part of Kate—I'd played a female snowman in my first-grade holiday play and worked my way up to interpretive speaking on the Pioneer speech team. I'd been a stand-in for one of the seniors in the school's *Little Shop of Horrors* production last year. And I had practiced my try-out lines in front of the mirror at least fifty times last week! No, expecting to do well seemed rational.

Maybe it was the competition? Brisa and Chris both got prestigious roles. But Joss had called Mrs. Hardcastle a lead, making my "success" actually bigger and better than theirs. I blew out a frustrated breath. "It has to be the guy, then," I said out loud.

Brisa snapped to attention. "What guy?"

The two of us were stretched out on the floor in my new living room at Worden's Woods, or "Dub-Dub," as Chris and I called the community. The place was both lavish and basic, a collection of manufactured homes that would be unremarkable anywhere else but on their foundations in the middle of a lovely old-growth forest with a tumbling creek running through it. Once the site of a logging camp and then a hippie commune, it was now a residential nature park, with duck ponds and waterfalls and two hundred-foot-tall trees surrounding the modest homes.

This location rivaled our last address, I thought, where my father, Pete Hall, still lived—two miles down the highway in a rural neighborhood, on a twelve-acre parcel that included a white, Colonial-style house, a rolling, green lawn, and more landscaping than was remotely necessary out in the country. My mom, Reza, could have taken the property in the divorce but had opted for less overhead and a better, more secure lifestyle. The new place had a fraction of the square footage but gave us two women the run of a vast, outdoor playground. Although my dad had scoffed at the location and it felt like a step down, I had to admit that it was fun moving to a new house. Plus the living room itself, with its floor-to-ceiling windows and thick, new carpeting, was a comfortable spot to hang out.

I heard panting. My black Lab, Teddy Roosevelt, padded through the room on his way out the back dog door and took his heavy breathing with him. I rolled over on the wheat-colored rug and considered my friend's question.

"Which guy?" Brisa asked again, more impatiently. "The one you don't know, or the one you can't stand?"

Hm.

"I guess it doesn't matter either way. Dean Dixon is not an option, and even if the other guy, Mason, *were* interested, there's nothing I can do about it. I'm romantically paralyzed."

"Come on, *chica*," Brisa brushed me off. "That's all in your head."

"In my head and somewhat lower in the rest of my body," I said ruefully. "Every time I even think about getting horny, Mom introduces me to some nice man she met on the CallMe website."

"Ugh." Brisa shuddered.

"There is no way I am dating at the same time my forty-one-year-old mother is dating. End of story."

"That *would* be a wrinkle in your cap," Brisa agreed. "Then again, it could help you with method acting. *Señora Hardcastle.*"

I reached over and slugged her. "Why do I have to be the old lady?" I whined.

Brisa mimicked me: "Why do I have to be the star?"

"Yeah, well, I don't consider it the star," I mumbled, sitting up cross-legged. "Malia's a star. Blaze is a star," I said, meaning Malia Kendrake as Kate and Blaze Heyden, the college girl playing Constance Neville.

Brisa softened her voice. "By the end of this production, honey, we'll all be stars." She sat up straight. "But how weird will it be to have Hamada as your *son?*"

I cringed. "My neighbor as Tony Lumpkin, Hardcastle's possibly bastard son born before her second marriage." A grin stole across my face. "It does have comedic possibilities."

"It could have far-reaching possibilities," Brisa remarked. "As your son, Chris will have to do as you say." She paused, then added devilishly, *"Whatever* you say."

"There is that." Some consolation. Although Chris generally complied with any reasonable suggestion. Maybe it was time to be unreasonable. "Meanwhile," I continued, "the guy I like, the one playing Spider Marlow, will be 'dating' my stage daughter, Kate. Holy crap! I'm creepy if I make a move on him, and he's creepy to everyone else if he makes a move on me. Which he won't. Because I'll be 'married' to the guy I don't like but have to pretend to like, or we'll never make it through six weeks of production!"

Brisa murmured in a comforting tone, "That is complicated. And bad luck. Because Dean Dixon, while a jerk, *es sabroso.*" She licked her fingertips. "Spider, on the other hand, while still yummy, looks like he has more going on upstairs." She tapped her head. When Mason Jones had tried out for the role of Marlow, the nickname "Spider" had immediately stuck. He wasn't really Brisa's type, but she could see the attraction. "Wouldn't your dad just croak if you hooked up with a guy named Spider?" She wiggled her eyebrows at me. "Good thing you can't possibly go out with anyone while your moms is doing it."

"Yeah." I swallowed. "Good thing."

***

By the time the first rehearsal rolled around on Tuesday afternoon, raw acceptance had set in. Any kid who has been through their parents' divorce knows what it's like to be stuck where you don't want to be: you either keep trying to derail reality, or you fold. And getting a starring role in a play wasn't as bad as all that. I guessed I could handle it. Besides, my friends were here. But where was Joss?

"You'd think the director could be on time," one of the servant girls grumbled. "Where the heck is she?"

"I saw her buttering up Mr. Casper over at Gregor Hall ," one of the stagehands said.

"Probably trying to change her Bio grade," someone guessed.

"She's gotta be flunking after spending all her time writing the script."

Dean Dixon had been sitting on the edge of the stage riser, browsing on his phone, but he looked up when he heard this. "Well, if that's true, then the show's dead meat. You've gotta keep a C average to do any extracurrics—or, at least, that's how it is at Foster. That's why I'm here. Extra credit for English, otherwise it's no sports for me."

I shot Brisa a look. That explained that. Why else would one of the sporting group want a part in our dog show?

Mason Jones, his hair pulled back in a ponytail today, made a show of checking a watch he wasn't wearing. In his Spider Marlow voice, he said, "I'm so pissed she's late! But I'm grateful she's not here."

Dave B. waved an arm at him and announced, "Both sides, ladies and gentlemen. Spider Marlow thinks he can have it both ways. But that's how you satisfy no one. A sure recipe for not getting laid."

I flushed at hearing the word *laid* while I was looking directly at Mason.

Chris, oblivious, sat down next to me in a folding chair. "Just like in the play, huh? Except, Spider eventually gets—"

"—gets the girl!" I supplied. *Not* laid.

"It's a quarter after! Where's Joss?" Malia demanded of nobody in particular. She summoned Brisa. "Hey, Second-in-command. Did she tell you she'd be late?"

My best friend did not like people to know that she did not know something. "I'm her cousin," Brisa said, "not her mother!" Then she stage-whispered into the wings, "Kavi? Did she tell you where she was going?"

Over the sound system came a hushed-yet-booming reply: "NO."

Some kids started running some lines. Five minutes went by. Then another ten.

"That's it. I've got better things to do," said one of the play's male servants, throwing his hands in the air.

"Me too," Dean said, untangling his long legs from the folding chair opposite himself that he'd propped them up on.

I looked up from the script I was following for Chris to see more people get ready to leave. "Breese?"

Brisa shrugged and picked up her own backpack.

What was all this? *"Hey!"* I yelled loud enough to make folks stop in their tracks. "Hang on a minute." I took the front of the stage. "We've still got over an hour. And we'll only have a dozen rehearsals. Why don't we just start practicing?"

Like the voice of God standing too close to the microphone, "GOOD IDEA" floated over the sound system.

I cut a look into the wings, but it was too dark to see anything but some pinpoint green lights from an obscure console. Brisa and Dean turned back, but the others continued up the ramp toward the doors.

"You might not want to go," came the amplified, disembodied, lilting voice again, more restrained this time, making them pause. "There. Will. Be. Pizza." Then silence.

Malia stomped over to the wings and yelled, "Kavi! I thought you said she didn't tell you where she went!"

The microphone clicked on again. "She left me a note."

Those who had wanted to go looked pissed, while Chris, Dean, and I got a chuckle out of it. So, this Kavi genius was the literal sort and knew how to use it. Interesting.

***

The aromatic mixture of tomato sauce, spices, and cheese drew every player back to rehearsal. All eyes were on Joss, who put three pizza boxes on an old set table, but didn't open them. The players milled around, waiting.

"Okay! I'm not sorry I'm late," Joss said, standing guard over the boxes. "I did that on purpose, by the way. Because we are a team, and you need to act like it."

Understanding was beginning to peek out of the dawn clouds for me.

Joss put her hands on her hips. "Now, who got impatient and tried to leave?"

Several arms raised.

"Who stayed?"

The rest of them raised their hands. Joss pointed at Brisa. "Why?"

Brisa said solemnly, "Because Carli said we should just start practice."

Joss singled out Mason. "Why?"

He paused. "Kavi said there would be pizza."

Above the buzz of laughter, Joss said, "Carli? Thanks for stepping up. That's what I'm talking about. You get the first slice." And she pulled the lid off the first pizza box. "Kavi? Come get yours."

He did, and he and I met over the steaming pie. Kavi was my height, a couple inches over five feet, but stockier. He moved softly over the wooden stage and met my eyes with his dark, hooded ones. Abruptly dropping his gaze and pushing his wire-rimmed glasses up on his nose, he said, "You first." We each took a slice, and then repaired to the folding chairs, Kavi moving away and taking a corner seat in the very back. Joss cleared the others to help themselves and get seated.

While they chewed and wiped greasy fingers on paper towels that someone had snagged from the bathroom, Joss laid down the rules. "Rehearsal begins on time and goes the full ninety minutes—more if we're in the middle of a breakthrough. If someone is late, including myself, designate a leader and carry on. If your stage partner is missing, grab someone from the crew to read their lines. We have 1,080 minutes until dress rehearsal. Let's use it."

Brisa was put in charge of logistics of every kind, including collecting cell phones.

"What!" Malia and Blaze reflexively clutched their phones to their chests, balancing gnawed pizza slices in their free hands as Brisa passed by with a locker room basket to gather the devices.

If Joss had been looking for the best way to gain people's attention, I thought, the combination of hot pizza and no phones was it. After all the freak-out rumors, the play schedule was pretty straightforward: we'd progress in stages and be ready for dress rehearsal before the end of the next month. There would be two practices a week, including one on Friday nights, with all lines in Act One expected to be memorized within two weeks.

Dean, sitting with the guy stars, heard this and started laughing. "We have to *know* all the lines? I'm more used to, like, ad-libbing."

Chris, sitting with me across from them, rolled his eyes. "It's a *play,* man. They don't call it rehearsal for nothing."

Joss ignored Dean's ignorance and said, "Get together with your stage partner outside of practice. You'll have your lines down in no time."

I gave Chris a withering look. *Great. I'm his tutor.*

"Now, if we're all fat and happy ... Mr. and Mrs. Hardcastle? You're up first."

I let my eyes widen to take in the expectant castmates surrounding me. *What the heck am I doing here?* There were some really good actors here, like Dave B. and Mason. What had been delicious pizza moments before became sand in a cement mixer inside me. *I could just leave.* But Dean got up from his chair with his script to join me, and Brisa directed us to a mark onstage, and then Joss called, "When you're ready!"

So, it was now or never.

One of the makeup crew was to read the stage directions today. She began, "'The time is Now, but the elders in this play are dressed in 1773 period costume, while the young people wear styles current to today. No mention is made of this disparity; it is allowed to simply bridge the gap between the two time periods and increase opportunities for humor. The place is the drawing room in a big, old-fashioned mansion.'"

Silence, for a moment, and another. Someone cleared their throat.

"Oh, m-me?" I stammered. "Yes."

I slid my eyes at Dean, but his were on his script. An actor, in the end, is alone onstage.

I took a deep breath and read, in a voice not quite my own, "'One vacation is all I ask, Mr. Hardcastle. The pandemic has subsided! Can we not take a little trip, to rub off the rust a little? I'm going stir-crazy in this old house.'"

A pause, and then Dean's broadcasting tenor recited, "'This ... *vintage* house, you mean, old girl. That's the telling—I mean, selling point for our future B&B. And what's the rush? It was just ... just months ago the CDC was begging each state to keep its own fools at home. Ah, solitude! Those were good times.'"

Mrs. Hardcastle was restless, so I let it rip in an old lady meets debutante tone. "Oh, sure, fine times indeed; for a recluse. Here we live in an old, rumbling mansion that looks for all the world like an inn, but we never see any company. Our only visitors are Online Eats and the Rainforest delivery guy. It's like a tomb in here. I hate the quiet! And the boredom."

Joss tossed in her approval. "Sounds natural, Carli! Go on, Mister H."

But Dean was still reading from a radio script, not really interpreting the words. "'Boredom.' I mean,

'Boredom? I love it. Boredom is underrated. You have to admit, Missus, I have been pretty satisfied with a boring ... old ... wife."

Old, was she? I took offense, and the Hardcastles bickered over who was the more ancient. Then Mister brought up his aging stepson—Missus's boy by her first marriage, Tony—as evidence of her advanced years.

I brushed this off. "That would be the fault of Mr. Lumpkin, my first husband," I laid the blame on the absent, deceased man. "He was old when Tony was born. It can't be me; the poor boy has not even come of age yet."

Without taking a humor beat, Dean read flatly, "'Nor ever, will I wager.' No—wait. 'Nor ever *will*, I wager." He looked over at Joss for confirmation, then went on, "When you're as immature as that boy, twenty-one is just a ... number.'" He wouldn't get a laugh for that, either.

I ignored the slight to my son. "No matter. Tony Lumpkin will have a good inheritance when he hits twenty-one, thanks to his dear, departed father. My son won't *have* to mature in order to spend fifteen hundred a month for life!"

Again, Joss encouraged me. "You're getting it! Come on, Dean. Show us where Hardcastle is coming from."

Eyes glued on the page, he simply raised the volume. "'You're as immature as he is.'"

This raised my hackles again. "Oh, now it's my fault? The poor boy suffered so from the divorce and then the funeral. It set him back a few grade levels. When he is old enough for college, I'm sure he'll man up soon enough."

Hardcastle, however, held little regard for the boy. I waited for Dean to shoot back a zinger, but again he just read from the page. "'College? No, no; if he ever graduates high school, a trip to the vape shop is the only higher learning he'll ever get.'"

I waited a beat to elicit a laugh from those listening, but just then, the stage went dark around me. Some pops and clicks came from the sound system. *Is there an electrical storm?*

I could sense Dean next to me, but couldn't discern his outline—the theater fixtures, all black, reflected no available light, if there was any in the windowless hall. "Er, Joss?" he said in his everyday tenor. "What now?"

Brisa called out, "Anybody backstage got a flashlight?"

There was no answer.

I shifted on my feet, and an empty plastic water bottle that someone had dropped crunched underneath me. Now I was afraid to move, afraid I might run into something or fall off the stage. I heard Chris's voice: "Anybody? Lights?"

"Kavi? Are you doing that?" My words sounded small in the darkness.

A soft-spoken response coming from just behind me startled me. "No. I'm right here. But I can't find my flashlight in the dark. If someone's got a phone, we can use the light on it to find the breaker."

We heard someone fumbling around onstage and then Brisa saying, "Hang on, here's one—"

She was interrupted by a loud swooshing sound; it seemed to sail through the sound system and right into my chest. "Kavi?" I called weakly, stomach churning and fear rising.

Then the sound effect disappeared, and a man's impatient, nasal voice barked, "Listen up!" Then a woman's sensual baritone pushed through the speakers. "Good afternoon. We are Loretta and Jack."

The house lights gradually came up to reveal Dean, Brisa, Kavi, Chris, and me onstage. Was this some kind of joke? We goggled at each other, and I peered wildly into the wings.

Where the hell did everyone else go?

"You five," came the dusky voice again. "You will do as we ask."

Chapter 3

My best friend did not like being told what to do by someone without the requisite authority. "Do what you ask?" Brisa retorted with more bravery than she could possibly be feeling. "I don't think so!"

The unfamiliar male voice with the high, nasal tone and *Get off my lawn* delivery, imitated Brisa's bravado through the theater sound system: "Don't make snap decisions!"

The owner of the dusky voice pointed out, "You don't even know the nature of our request."

"And what might that be?" Brisa demanded.

The rest of us stood there, stock still.

"All in good time," the voice purred.

I felt like I had to back Brisa up. "We don't have a lot of time," I said. "We're in the middle of rehearsal."

"Well, if you want to resume that activity," the voice continued, "you'll first *satisfy* our request." This last bit came with a sexy innuendo added.

Brisa wasn't cajoled. "Look, Loretta, or whatever your name is—"

"I'm *Jack*," the sexy lady's voice informed her. "He's Loretta."

"But I thought—"

"Don't assume!" Loretta's scolding voice was higher-pitched but still the more male-sounding one. "In your understanding, I'm a *he*," Loretta explained. "Jack's a *she*. But you can forget all that, because our kind don't do gender."

"Well, do you do bodies?" came Dean's measured broadcasting speech. I looked over my shoulder, having forgotten he was there. "Why don't you show yourselves, and we'll talk?"

"*Bodies.*" Jack gave a low, slow chuckle. "That is so last millennium."

Dean exchanged a slightly worried look with me, and Kavi spoke up. He'd been so quiet that I'd forgotten he was onstage as well. "If you don't mind my asking," he said demurely, "how is it that you've tapped into my PA system? I unhooked the amplifier while I was making some repairs."

"We'll ask the questions," grumpy Loretta snapped. "If we like what we hear, we may ask for your input."

Jack continued evenly, "If we are satisfied by your input, then we will release you to continue doing ... whatever it is that you do."

Brisa didn't like these new rules. "No deal." She scooped up her backpack and motioned to the rest of us. "Come on, guys. Let's get out of here."

Jack warned ominously, yet sexily. "You might not want to leave."

"Why? We already had our pizza," I retorted. I was torn, but hey. We were here, and they weren't. What were they going to do to stop us?

I walked over and tapped Chris on the arm. We followed Brisa down the stage stairs, and Kavi and Dean moved after us.

"Well, then," Jack said with a sigh, "you leave us no choice."

All at once, the floor and walls fell away. I was not alone in my stark, sudden screaming. I pinwheeled my arms, reaching out to my castmates to try and stop what felt like a drop through infinity. I could feel wind whistle past my ears and hear everyone else's uncontrollable shouts. Just as my stomach was about to lurch right up through the top of my head, my feet felt something solid beneath them, and the movement ceased.

Covered in icy sweat, I caught sight of Chris, then Brisa nearby. I hazarded a glance at my feet ... and wished I hadn't.

Inches from my shoes was the edge of some sort of rocky ground, with too much open space in front of it. Taking that in, I realized I stood on a cliffside, with a towering drop-off before me, and far below, an undulating body of water—a swiftly running river that tossed white water around the pointed tops of jagged rocks. Instinctively, I reached backward and pressed my hands against something firm to steady myself, maybe a rock wall.

"Shit!"

I couldn't tell whose voice that was—it could've been Chris's or Brisa's, or my own. My knees buckled, and one foot skidded forward.

A hand gripped my wrist. It was Kavi's; the touch of this near-stranger was as comforting to me in that suspended moment as a mother's love. He said nothing as my wild eyes found his, full of disbelief.

Then, off to my left, a torrent of swearing poured forth in Spanish, and I translated what I could into English: *where, place, mother,* and something about putting shit back up someone's ass.

I had a feeling that cursing was not going to save us right now. Through teeth gritted like I'd contracted tetanus, I stage-whispered, "B.! These people mean business. *¡No es la hora para soltar tacos!*"

Above the rushing sound of water and dwindling screams from our group came Jack's husky chuckle. "Letting 'tacos' fly is no way to solve one's problems, it's true. Let's keep it clean, shall we?"

Loretta sounded even more perturbed than before. "These humanoids are so predictable! Their first instinct is to projectile-vomit something out of their mouths." He softened his acerbic tone. "But I like this one. Carli-Person!" His voice seemed to attach itself to the inside of my head as he addressed me. "You've got better self-control than most," he said.

"M-me?" I croaked, eyes fixed on the water far below, wrist still gripped by Kavi, legs still weak.

Jack *tch*ed at her counterpart. "But the other one is their leader."

Loretta barked a nasal laugh. "I don't think so." He paused. "Let's find out." Then he said to me, as though this were some sort of focus group, "What's the biggest problem facing your world?"

Frantic Chris was tired of waiting for explanations. He broke in, "You mean, other than teetering on a cliff, about to fall to our deaths? Can we get down from here first?" His voice rose and cracked at the end.

Then Dean announced, "We are not from your planet," as though speaking to a child. "I'm Dean. I'm in charge here. You can talk to me." His radio voice sounded reassuring to me, but it didn't work on our unseen captors.

"I'm talking to this one!" Loretta shrieked. "This Carli-Person! Not this Dean, or this Chris, or this Brisa, or this Kavi."

Chris mumbled at us, "How the hell do they know our names?"

This seemed to have put the real fear into Brisa, on top of what was already there. She started mumbling the Lord's Prayer in Spanish.

"Well!" Chris exclaimed, confronting her. "I can see *you* won't be of any help to us."

"On the contrary," Jack purred. "You will each be of help to each other. Or there will be no going back to your little play-acting." She let this sink in. "Now. When a team needs a plan, a team needs a leader. What are the options? What's the consensus? How will the plan be executed?"

This shut up Brisa's praying. "Please. Do *not* say *executed* right now!"

Jack and Loretta ignored her and pressed me once more instead.

Loretta called in a singsong manner, "*Car*-li?"

"What's the world's biggest problem, as you see it?" Jack repeated.

Talk about being put on the spot. I couldn't think straight, much less answer trick questions. I balanced on the edge of a cliff, staring at deadly rocks and raging water, with all of my friends terrified and ready to lose it. Suddenly, my foot slipped again, and Kavi's grip on my wrist tightened. I heard the distinct crackle of thin plastic and felt that damn water bottle crush flat under my shoe. But I didn't dare move or try to kick it off the ledge. Fear gave way to anger.

"Trash! Okay? Garbage pollution! Crap piling up all over the place!" That was true of how this day was going, anyway.

"That's not bad," Jack said casually to her counterpart.

"It'll do for now," Loretta admitted in his reedy voice. "Your choice, Carli-Person. You can see how easily plastic waste makes its way from rivers like this one to the sea, where gulls and dolphins and whales end up choking on it. Big threat to the food chain, of which you are a part. High stakes. You can die now, or you can die later. So, what are you gonna do about it?"

Now? I'm supposed to solve the global litter problem on the side of a fricking precipice? With what, my good looks?

I scanned the terrified faces of my friends: Dean, hopeful; Kavi, inscrutable; Chris, willing me to say the right thing; Brisa, wishing for divine intervention. I scratched for what remained of my composure and considered the question.

Back when I lived on Jude Road and walked my dog, Teddy, I'd picked up a lot of roadside trash. It was something to do as we went along, and the never-ending stream of tossed fast-food containers, beer cans, and other junk was a magnet for my always-hungry Labrador retriever. He even started spotting litter first. He'd fix on it, and I'd pick it up, depositing the handful or poop bag of stuff at the next garbage can down the road and giving him a "Good boy!" But that had all ended when we moved. At Dub-Dub, there were signs all over saying, $500 fine for littering, and they meant it. I could count the pieces of contraband I'd come across in the last few months on one hand.

So, I was a little rusty. To think about one empty plastic bottle, or thousands, or millions winding up in a whale's stomach was revolting, but what the heck could someone like me do about that? I guessed that's what Loretta and Jack wanted to know.

Okay. What I'd do first is ask people smarter and more knowledgeable than me for their ideas. Then ask everyday people what they'd be willing to do. Next, I'd take all the responses and find the best ones. Then I'd figure out how to do those things and, I guessed, pay for them. Then I'd enlist folks to actually get that done.

Again, my foot slipped on the slick, crumpled plastic and slid nearer the edge. *Holy shit!*

My sloshing stomach dove, seeming to drop over the side of the embankment like a half-full water bottle on its way to the sea, leaving my breath heaving in my chest. All available eyes were on me, as though I had an answer, as though I was the one who could save us. This just wasn't fair! I dropped my gaze, then tried to will that empty water bottle away from its watery trash can.

"*Well?* Carli-Person?" Loretta prompted me again. "I said, what're you gonna do about it?" he taunted me.

This was nuts.

I snapped. "You want to know what I'm gonna do? Do you?" As anger clouded my thoughts, I leaned forward against Kavi's firm grip, reached down, and scooped up the bottle. "I'm gonna pick it up!"

***

The next thing I knew, my feet were trodding the boards of the stage once more. *Good answer,* I said to myself; then, the following second, *What the fuck just happened?*

Before I could answer that, a query sailed from the wings: "Where the hell is Mr. Lumpkin? Tony? You're on!"

A speechless Dean waved a speechless Chris over to the mark near me. We all looked like we'd seen ten thousand ghosts and had sex with them.

"Line!" Joss was getting pissed. "Where's my AD?"

Brisa was standing fixed next to the stage-right wing, literally babbling. It didn't sound like Spanish or English. Maybe those ... *aliens* had given her one of those universal translators.

Getting nothing from her, Joss yelled, "Mr. Hardcastle! Exit!"

Dean just stood there stupidly. *Cut him some slack, babe,* I thought. For all we knew, the man had just permeated the space/time barrier.

The offstage cast and crew started getting restless in their seats. Joss asked Kavi for a microphone, but he faded into the wings and didn't return. Now Joss started letting the tacos fly, and somehow, her determined cursing brought me back to the present.

Noting the script in my hand, where it was supposed to be, I moved closer to Chris. Just then, my foot came down on the cast-off water bottle. *C-runch!*

I skidded on it, losing my balance and scarecrowing my arms out. I fell forward anyway, right into Dean's midsection—the dude was tall—and he caught me with both arms, with a *pop!*, like I was a line drive. The sound was loud enough to get everyone else's attention. Even the swearing stopped. You could've heard a tortilla drop.

When I looked over the stage, I didn't see an integrated theater cast and crew—I saw some bored people sitting in folding chairs, two pissed-off women trying to hold their tongues, and a few shell-shocked high school kids wondering what to do onstage. That was a problem. And the only way to fix it, like any disaster that happened during a performance, was to just keep going like nothing had happened.

I opened my mouth and strangled out, in a voice slightly higher than my regular one, "T-Tony?" I cleared my throat, checking the script. "Where are you going, my charmer? Won't you give Papa and I a little company?"

Chris's eyes were pasted on mine.

I whispered, "It's 'Out, Mother; I've got a date.'"

After an eon, he repeated the line. I was back in Mrs. Hardcastle's skin, so I asked him if the date was with a girl or a boy. This finally snared Chris's awareness. He grinned and read, in a hurried manner, as though to shut down further questions, "'Just friends, Ma! And DJ Tom Twist will be there tonight, spinning the platters and laying down the beat.'" He pantomimed that and simulated a beatbox puff and buzz. The scene closed with Tony refusing to stay home and the two of us exiting.

Dean found his voice and said to Chris, "Nice hip-hop move!" while Joss called it a day. She thanked me in front of everyone for stepping in with the line and announced that that was how it's done.

A warm glow flowed in where cold sweat had been not so long before. The back-and-forth was jarring. My whole body felt like it was riddled with holes— like I was stuck in some sort of cosmic acupuncture session. It was weird, but I had never felt more *alive.* My fingers closed around the script in my hand, and I squeezed it hard to make sure I was here, now, where I was supposed to be.

While everyone else filed out of the theater, the five of us were all looking a little out-of-body as we gravitated to one another, falling back to wait for Kavi, who had emerged from the wings and was the last to leave. He snapped off all the lights except those in the entryway. We pushed up the ramp toward the door, and I looked over my shoulder at the now-black box of a stage. Remembering something, I broke away from them and ran back there, feeling around on the floor near the footlights.

"What th—?" Brisa saw what was in my hand when I jogged up to them.

"I didn't want to leave *this,*" I said ruefully, raising the squashed plastic lump and then shoving it in my bag.

"You'd better recycle that," Chris said somberly.

"Is someone going to explain what happened?" Dean asked as we made it to the hallway and headed toward the building exit.

"Who can?" Chris said, expecting no answer.

Brisa made the sign of the cross and whispered, *"Fueron espíritus."*

"Spirits? I was thinking aliens," I said, as though I thought that all the time. "But I kind of doubt it. What's your take, Kavi?"

Kavi hesitated, shifting his overstuffed backpack to his other shoulder. His gold-rimmed glasses caught the overhead fluorescents and shot a reflected ray of light in my eye. He actually noticed this and ducked his head. "I have several ... takes."

Brisa burst through the outside door, and Dean held it open for the rest of us.

"Thank you," Kavi said, blinking in the late-afternoon sunlight. "Do you want to hear my theories?"

Did I? "Sure."

He set his heavy backpack down on the sidewalk. "One is that an elaborately staged charade was played on us. Someone could rig a micro-amplifier to a remote mike and slip speakers into our belongings. Then they could broadcast some sound effects, use a projection screen to re-create a very lifelike outdoor set, and then reverse the whole thing when they were done. Of course, that doesn't take into account—"

"I don't buy it," Dean said bluntly. "What's your next idea?"

Kavi ducked his head again and obeyed. "We were abruptly acquainted with the limits of physics and the limitlessness of quantum mechanics, allowing us to dematerialize from this place and re-form from subatomic particles in another place, and possibly another time. Although, having done so, I would note that there existed in that time/space an item from our present plane that would seem to indicate the persistence of the litter problem, the conduit from stream to ocean, and the human cause of said problem—"

Dean cut him off again. "That sounds far-fetched."

Chris raised his eyebrows and said drolly, "Quantum mechanics is inherently far-fetched."

"Thank you," Kavi told him in a clipped voice, miffed at the aspersion cast on his plausible theory.

Brisa had been listening to these rationales intently, perhaps hoping to hear of something more normal than the presence of spirits behind their encounter. "Got anything else?" she asked him, since he did seem to know what he was talking about, even if it didn't make any sense.

Kavi looked at her through his lenses. "Hypnotism. Mass hypnotism. Although why only the five of us would be chosen, I do not know. But I have some more theories about that...."

I gave Chris a *Do you believe this guy?* look.

"...and yet, I do not know which one of them is correct, or, in fact, if any of them are, and if so, why I did not predictably see that coming, because if I had, I might have been able to prevent such a fright, but then I...." He sensed that he was rambling on and should stop. "I am simply not sure if any of those possibilities is relevant to what just happened at rehearsal," he ended, somewhat breathless.

So were the rest of us. I was having trouble breathing, and I know my mind was spinning. I also knew I liked this guy.

"Well, Kavi," I said slowly, "you were right about one thing."

"What is that?"

I grinned. "There was pizza."

Chapter 4

A little rain didn't dilute the color palette of the Dub-Dub forest that Chris, Teddy Roosevelt, and I walked through two days later, after school. Wasabi-green frills dotted the tops of several sawed-off tree stumps, likely cut down after damage by February's ice storm. The reddish bark of cedars shot upward from beds of darker-green sword ferns and shamrock-shaped oxalis that lined the roadside and hiking areas. A rust-orange dwelling was reflected upside-down in one of the placid, turquoise duck ponds that spread out below us, as the road we were on rose up into the foothills. It literally smelled like spring.

Suddenly, Teddy lunged after a ground squirrel that burst from the bushes and crossed the pavement right in front of us. He gave a yelp, and I hung onto his leash like a water skier, used to it. The dog stopped and shook rainwater from his shiny, black body, some landing on my rain jacket. "What if we did that?" I invited Chris to imagine people sloughing off unwanted liquids and debris.

"Then we'd be the ones on leashes," Chris replied.

"We *were* the ones on leashes the other day. Are we even gonna talk about that?" My body recalled the sensation of feeling perforated by its unprecedented movement, and I shuddered.

"No," Chris joked.

The five of us actually had not done so yet. B. had avoided the topic during gym class on the jogging track, and Dean had never texted me about running lines, so I hadn't seen him either. Because our next rehearsal wasn't until tomorrow night, I had not run across Kavi, an exchange student at the college who was getting some prerequisites out of the way for a course of study in engineering, Chris had said. They'd chatted before practice on Pizza Day and found out they both spoke Nerd, or something. But none of us had discussed the unexplainable, and I couldn't hold out any longer.

"I wonder if Kavi's made any progress on his theories," I began as we descended the high hill toward an off-road trail.

Chris kicked a few pieces of gravel ahead of us. "Kavi... He hit on something with that *Why just us five?* thing. After listening to those two weirdos order us around, I still have no clue."

"A sexy chick with no body, and a guy named Loretta that sounds like someone's angry grandpa... What would they want with us?"

"Maybe the play has something to do with it. They did sound like a couple of megalomaniac directors, trying to move us around on the world stage."

"They couldn't be more different from Joss, though," I pointed out. "I don't suppose Brisa's told her anything about the ... incident."

"No way," Chris said as we followed the sign to the left that read walking trail.

Teddy Roosevelt eagerly plunged into a thicket off to one side, dragging me with him until I hauled us both forward again.

Chris already knew Brisa well, I thought. I'd introduced them a few months before, when Mom and I had moved to Dub-Dub and B. started coming over in the afternoons so one of her sisters would have to babysit their little brother. Brisa would never admit she couldn't explain something, and if she couldn't fabricate some plausible rationale, she'd pretend like it didn't exist. Which wasn't a bad tactic in this case, it seemed to me. They say the Lord works in mysterious ways, but this sure wasn't one of them. I didn't know what to think.

Gravel crunched beneath our shoes as we followed Teddy on his taut leash single file down the slope past conifers and underbrush, the moisture from the wet plants painting further shine on his black coat. He stopped to sniff something at the base of one of the old logging contraptions that were strewn around the property as lawn ornaments. This one looked like something out of a steampunk video game.

"So, here's a question," I tossed over my shoulder. "What about tomorrow night? Are you planning to show?"

"Rehearsals are mandatory," Chris said, "so I guess so. But what about the rest of us? Brisa looked scared out her wits. Dean, I dunno."

"He's a little ... simple. Like, I wonder if it even registered with him that we basically time traveled. Or space traveled. Or, at least, *traveled.*"

We reached the foot of the rise and stopped to let Ted pee on a fence post.

"Guy like him?" Chris said. "I doubt if he believes in anything he can't see. Unlike Brisa, with her *Santería* and Jesus to fall back on. Talk about two ends of the spectrum." He paused. "Nice guy, though, Dixon. He did give us all a ride home."

I recalled the gesture, soon after we'd heard Kavi's hypotheses in the community college parking lot. Dean told us to wait there, and a few moments later drove up in a black Jeep, one of those muscular ones with more bulk on the outside than room on the inside. Brisa had called shotgun, so I squeezed in back, in between the two other guys. Outside of providing directions, Kavi had been silent all the way to his hosts' home. Oddly, B. hadn't said a word, either, before Chris and I had exited the vehicle at Worden's Woods.

"So, what *is* your explanation for all this, Hamada? If you're somewhere between heavenly beings and quantum physics."

"I'm all for following the science," he said. "But we have no evidence yet."

"I'm pretty sure I don't *want* any more evidence," I grumbled, remembering the plastic bottle souvenir that I'd left in my backpack. It was real, and it was still there; I'd checked. "Okay, how about this: why the weird question about global problems, and why did 'the directors' ask me?"

Chris was quiet for a moment, and we started walking again along the lower road that skirted the duck pond. "That looks to be the main thing, doesn't it?" he murmured. "The fact that you didn't answer the question definitively but they released us anyhow suggests that: a) you're supposed to keep on thinking about that, and/or b) they aren't done with us yet."

This last bit brought me up short, and I stopped so abruptly at the edge of the pond that a raft of tiny frogs leapt from their hiding spots on the bank into the pond mud, with indignant squeaks. "But ... I did pick up the bottle. That *was* the answer."

"How do you keep an empty bottle from reaching the sea? It's a little more complicated than just picking it up." Chris wagged a finger at me. "I have a feeling, Carli, that that was only the beginning of the answer."

***

I did get a text from Dean Dixon later that day, asking me to help him memorize his lines, but I had homework to do. I agreed to meet him before Friday rehearsal, meaning I'd have to scarf down some dinner, walk the dog, and get the bus to the college before five p.m. I hoped I'd get some karma points for that.

I was somewhat queasy thinking of spending one-on-one time with Dean, but my trepidation grew the closer I got to the theater. My remedial costar was probably the least of my problems; I did not know what was going to happen to me onstage, and I wasn't sure I could go through another death-defying incident. Maybe, as Kavi said, it was just a joke. Somebody had their fun, and now we could get on with the play production.

I was relieved to find our sound and light honcho in the theater, puttering around with some wires in the half-light backstage. So, I wouldn't be alone—either with Dean or with our unseen "friends." Good. "Hey, Kavi," I called. He just nodded and went back to his work.

Dean strolled in about a quarter after—late—and walked right past me to see what Kavi was doing.

"K-Man," he greeted the stage engineer, "what's up with the repairs? Is that amp still giving you grief? Need some help?" Kavi shrugged him off, but Dean wouldn't accept his reserve. "This looks a little like my broadcast booth. Sure you can't use an extra hand?"

Kavi sighed and said, "Okay. Hand me that electrician's tape over there."

Dean hopped to where he was pointing and fetched it.

I crossed my arms, pissed. Why were guys more interested in mechanics than people? How did they expect to ever hook up with anybody? Not that I wanted that anybody to be me, but just in general. For an entire sex that claimed to be obsessed with sex, they spent an awful lot of time on nuts and bolts.

The two guys huddled over some sort of switch that was on the fritz until I cut them off. "Hey! Mr. Hardcastle. I'm doing you a favor. You've got about ten seconds before I give up and go get some food." I'd only had time to slop down some cereal in order to make the bus here.

Dean deigned to glance my way. He looked like he was weighing the options for his attention. "Maybe Joss will be late again and there will be pizza."

"Maybe Joss will find a new male lead when you can't recite any of your lines." I blinked out an angry SOS.

This sank in. "Sorry, man," Dean said to Kavi. "Gotta get that extra credit for English."

Under his breath, Kavi said to no one in particular, "*Uri baba.* How is it that an English-speaking student cannot pass a high school English class?"

It was a reasonable question from someone fluent in both English and Bengali, and possibly other languages. But he let it go unanswered as Dean obediently followed me over to two folding chairs to run through our lines.

I was counting on repetition to get through his thick skull. Today, we went through our first scene twice, then moved on to Hardcastle's next scene with his daughter, Kate, whose lines I picked up.

Dean began reading in his radio voice, with no hint of Hardcastle's demeanor. "'Now, there's my pretty darling Kate! My own daughter, coming of age nicely, although a penchant for fashion is somewhat troubling.'"

I read off the stage direction: "'Enter Miss Hardcastle, dressed in a revealing top and tight leggings.'"

So did Dean: "'Hardcastle gasps.'"

I put down my script. "Jesus, Dean. Can you just do what it says? *You* gasp. It's called acting."

He gave an exaggerated inhale. "'Kate! Is that a new tattoo—of a clergyman having sex with—"

It just about killed me to speak as Kate, but I put on a rebellious-teen sort of voice. "God, Dad. Get with it. It's skin art. And you know our agreement. You let me put what I want on my body, and I'll cover it up when company comes over."

Him, reading in the same old generic tone: "'Well, we'll soon have more visitors than ever, once your mother and I secure the permit to run our B&B. Meanwhile, I'll expect you to honor that agreement this very evening.'"

Kate, skeptically: "Why? You mean, you've decided to rejoin the real world and invited someone over for a change?"

Him: "'I'll be plain with you, Kate. I've asked a friend's son over, and I think you'll find him *very* interesting. He'll be staying overnight, and his father intends to follow shortly after.'"

Kate, outraged: "You've set me up? A blind date? It's a thousand to one I won't like him; or he won't like me; or we both won't like each other."

Him: "'Give it a chance, child. Young Spider Marlow is the son of my old friend, Senator Charles Marlow, of whom you have heard me talk so often.

The young gentleman is bound for law school and plans a political career. [Frowns.]'"

I stopped. "You don't say *frowns*. You do it," I reminded him with little patience. "Come on, Dean. Think like a Hardcastle. Then say it that way. Now: think about Spider. Come on. '...bound for law school and plans a political career.' Like you're selling the blind date."

This hit home with him, and he put a little commercial spin on the line, then twisted his face as though trying to calculate the square root of something. This could be construed as a frown. "Spider?" he ad-libbed, then read, "'He'll need a new nickname, though.'"

"Better. Let's go on."

The father and daughter discuss the benefits of dating a guy with some political clout. Hardcastle is obviously thinking about a business permit, while Kate wanted some help with multiple parking tickets and a driver's license suspension. Besides the legal angle, Mister assures Miss that the boy is also supposed to be quite the stud.

This pleases Kate. "My dear Papa, say no more, he's mine!" My eyes widened at the stage direction. I reached for Dean's hand and kissed it.

He didn't break character, because he'd never been *in* character. "'But, Kate,'" he read, "'his father says young Marlow is one of the most bashful and reserved young fellows in the world. You'd better go upstairs and change into something more ... sedate.'"

Kate reacts to this word as though it were overcooked Brussels sprouts. "Eh! you have frozen me to death again. The need to be *sedate* has cancelled out the rest of his accomplishments. He sounds like a loser."

"'On the contrary, modesty usually indicates further noble virtues.'"

Kate considers the trade-off. "Modesty? Well, that's strike one. However, if he is everything else you mention, I believe he'll do still. As long as he has an 'in' with the DMV."

As the scene ended, by complete accident, Dean delivered Hardcastle's clueless response as it should have been, largely because he was clueless. "Huh?"

"That's it!" I said, reaching over and squeezing his knee. "Breakthrough, Dixon. Try to stay in Hardcastle's head like that."

"Like what?"

"Exactly like that." The key to this character was his obtuseness. All Dean had to do was be himself. Wouldn't Joss be pleased?

***

The rest of the cast and crew showed up by six, so Dean and I had to quit. "Next time," I warned, "we do the same thing without the notes. So, go home and practice after practice."

"I'll be working out after practice."

"So, say your lines while you do that. The gym has a mirror. You can work on that frown of yours."

He didn't commit to any of it. But he did sit with B., Chris, and me in the "offstage" onstage area while the girls went through the rest of the scene that focused on Kate and her cousin Constance—"Stanzi," for short.

Malia had taken her role to heart. She had dyed her hair three colors and cut some of it at an angle, and she was dressed to incite a riot. Interpreting Kate much as I had, as a defiant teen, she began, "Stanzi! Check it out: I've got a new coolie tat! Dad hates it. How do you think it looks?" She pulled her shoulder strap away from her top to reveal the art.

"Dang," Dean said. "She went and got inked for the part!"

"I don't think it's a real tattoo," Brisa whispered.

"Not bad for a temporary," I had to admit. I could actually make out a robed man doing it to someone, or something.

Blaze, as Miss Neville, wore her blonde hair down and her regular clothes but added some upper-class snoot to her voice. Constance learns of Kate's blind date and immediately recognizes who it is: "Spider Marlow?"

"The son of Senator Chuck Marlow," Kate informs her.

This confirms Miss Neville's suspicions. "There can't be two Spider Marlows.... He's got to be the best friend of Beau Hastings, my boo! They're roommates. Maybe you've seen him when we visited their dorm. Spider's a different sort of guy—he plays it straight for his father and the profs, so he can get the Benjamins and the grades. But after hours, he's a wild man." To herself, she said, "I've never seen anyone drink hand sanitizer before."

This got a laugh from everyone on and offstage. Having fallen out of character, the two women took a pause to regroup.

I was starting to relax. I had made it through my own date with Dean Dixon and wouldn't have to perform again until Act Two. We were all still required to follow every line in every scene, in case someone needed a stand-in or, as Joss said, "In case the cast suffers a 'unifying moment' of utter failure and one of you must step in to save the performance." In other words, if someone blew a line, any one of us should be able to jump in, ad-lib, and fix the mistake.

That I could do, I thought. As long as I were here to do it. And the further into our ninety-minute rehearsal we got, the better I felt about the odds of that happening. Until something else happened.

"Kavi," Joss called to him in the wings, "can we get a spot on these two?"

Without a word, the spot came up on Blaze and Malia.

Then it shifted to the corner that I sat in with my friends.

"Kavi? On the marker?"

But the focus widened to include Kavi over at his console, where he tried frantically to reposition the spot, to no avail. That left the five of us bathed in stage light. And everyone else was just ... gone.

I had only that moment to anticipate what came next.

The theater went black, and a man's barbed, staccato voice called, "Carli-Person! Come on. We're going on a trip. Bring your friends."

Chapter 5

I'd heard that travel broadens the mind, but this was ridiculous. Leaving the black box behind, my four friends and I appeared to be parachuting high above some wilderness area. In my sudden shock at the change of scenery, I took inventory of my parts. Arms, legs, working, but not doing any work. I had lost control of my body yet was safely coasting along at altitude, with Brisa and Chris on one side, and Dean and Kavi on the other. Our limbs were spread as though to catch the air, and I idly gave thanks that it wasn't raining. Or snowing.

Unable to adjust my position, I felt my eyes widen to saucers, trying to catch sight of everything that I'd never seen before—which was everything, at least at this height. I saw a steep, green mountainside with tiny dots that must be houses spilling across it, wisps of fog obscuring portions of the view beneath me. We banked, and off in the distance, the sloping foothills met the sea, with long, orange rays pushing the sun over the horizon. My mind tried to reconcile what I was seeing with why and how I was seeing it, but got nowhere. I would have screamed, but it didn't seem worth it.

Brisa had that covered. If any of the guys were making much noise, it couldn't be heard over what sounded like one long, Mexican-accented scream. It bounced back and forth between a single nonsyllable and a mixture of Spanglish curses and prayers. I looked over at the guys to see if their mouths were moving. I couldn't see Dean's face, but he shook as though he were shivering. Was it cold up here? Kavi appeared to be chanting something, and a mask of wonder showed Chris to be more enthralled than anything else. He cocked his head at me and raised his eyebrows.

We hurtled toward the mountain summit, but curiously, I felt no wind resistance or even the sensation of moving fast, just saw how quickly we were covering ground, or should I say, air.

"¡Dios mío!" yelled Brisa at my left elbow. She also held that classic freefall parachutist pose, as though gently resting on an undulating magic carpet of air.

"You rang?" came Loretta's voice in my head and, I assumed, my friends'.

"*Dios?* Oh, now we're supposed to call you 'God'?" I retorted before I even realized I could speak.

"I've got another name for him," Chris muttered.

How was I hearing anything? *Oh, like that's more important than how I'm flying over a mountain.* And now I was arguing with myself!

"Look," I said to Loretta. "How about telling us who you people are? If we're going to be together for a while."

Loretta barked a chuckle. "'People.'"

Jack said breezily, "We are who you think we are. If you think that's people, so be it."

Dean found his voice and spoke up. "Control freaks, I'm thinking. What do you plan to do with us?"

"That depends on what you do," Jack explained, as if we should all have known that.

"So..." Chris offered, "we act, you direct kind of thing?"

"Bingo."

"Now," Loretta's cranky voice took over, "does anybody recognize where we are?"

We had crested the mountaintop and now faced a large body of water, but in between lay a big, brown blob of land. I had no idea what that was.

Kavi, though, did. "This is Kolkata," he answered, excitement evident in his voice, "West Bengal state."

"We're fucking flying over *India?*" Chris exclaimed.

"Now, now. Let's keep it clean," Jack scolded him.

"Excuse me," he said. "Hey, Kavi, that's a city in there?" He was referring to the brown blob.

"Two rivers," Kavi said. "Look behind: the Ganges. Look below: the Hooghly. Plain as day. City of Kolkata."

"I don't want to look down!" Brisa yelled, but we all looked. Our bodies seemed able to respond as the directors wanted them to, but nothing more.

Yes, it was as Kavi said. Two rivers, to our eyes, just two wiggly lines—one thick with switchbacks, one thin with a more direct flow, and alongside that one, a brown city, if our friend was to be believed.

He went on happily, "We visit Nana and Nanī there each year. Well, except for the previous two years of the pandemic, and of course, this year I will not be going, as I will be engaged in my studies here and must make a brief trip to London, to see Ma and Baba."

I suddenly knew 100 percent more about Kavi's family than I had known. Before, it was like he had just been cultivated in the FCC petri dish and wound up in the theater.

"That's nice, Kavi," I said.

"Love London," Dean put in. "We flew to Heathrow and spent a few days in the city on our way to the French Alps." His voice thinned as he eyed the rapidly approaching brown city. "We never made it to Calcutta, though."

Kavi said something to himself in Bengali that made Loretta laugh. "And they say America is a classless society," the director answered sarcastically.

"I see the same classes," Kavi put in softly, "only differently arranged."

"Now," Loretta began again, addressing Kavi. "Since your leader, Carli-Person, needs some help with her little problem, it's up to you to shed some light."

There was a pause as we zoomed closer to the blob and began to make out the silhouette of a city beneath the brownish haze.

Jack prompted Kavi, "Do you have any light to shed?"

I threw Kavi a look that told him I suspected this was a continuation of our earlier dilemma. This was confirmed when that damn plastic bottle materialized in the sky in front of me, taunting us with its transparent, crumpled skin.

Kavi still hesitated, so Loretta, impatient as usual, snapped at him, "Knock, knock!"

Kavi whispered, "Who's there?"

"What do this bottle, the Ganges, and the Bay of Bengal all have in common?"

It sounded like a bad joke, but Kavi dutifully answered, "They all wind up in the ocean."

"Bingo," Jack said again. "Tell the man what he's won, Loretta."

In a fake announcer's voice, he said, "You've won an all-expenses paid trip to the shoreline!"

Brisa, who had stopped screaming a while back, now perked up. "The beach?" she clarified.

"If that's what you'd call it."

We descended in one motion, now only a few stories above sea level, or river level, as it turned out, amid a thick blanket of smog that made it difficult to breathe. In one pocket of the curving bank, the sand appeared to be moving. But as we got closer, I saw that it was the river itself, littered with refuse of all shapes and colors. And the smell was ... both ripe and rotten at the same time. I watched "my" plastic bottle sail into the mess.

"Oh, my," Kavi exclaimed. "It seems as though the latest litter campaign has not been successful."

"Understatement!" Dean shouted as we hurtled toward the sea of crap.

I watched as Brisa instinctively reached out a hand and he took it in midair. "This sweater is 'dry clean only'!" she wailed.

The fetid river seemed to rise up to meet us, and in that instant, the feeling and movement returned to my appendages. I started flapping my arms backwards in a wild attempt not to land there. "Jack! Loretta! You are *not* gonna drop us in that!"

And I turned out to be right. Just before gravity would get the best of me, my descent slowed, and little by little I neared the shore until, finally, my tippy-toes touched wet sand. I cringed, anticipating the feel of a slushy stream of garbage beneath my feet. All I felt was sand. And the river of refuse was gone.

***

"But how can this be?" I heard Kavi ask incredulously as I surveyed our immediate surroundings. I wondered, too, because everything seemed ... *clearer.* Looking up, I realized that the bank of smog was also gone. Kavi murmured something in Bengali in a tone of voice that perfectly expressed my surprise at the quick change, as though the environment had put on a new dress.

Brisa stumbled over and hugged me, and I hugged her back. "I'm so scared, Carli. How will we ever get home now?"

I wasn't used to this non-confident Brisa. "We'll just do as they say, *chica,*" I reassured her. I'd done it once; I could do it again.

Chris stood nearby, his spidey senses clearly tingling. That guy loved to take apart a problem and put it back together. Why hadn't the directors made him the leader?

Along the riverside, a half dozen people were combing the bank for debris and putting what they found in round bins on wheels. Dean had landed in their midst, but they ignored him, intent on their work. He stomped over to us from the water's edge and threw his head back, addressing our unseen captors. "You there! I've got my first batting practice tomorrow. You know, back in *America*. What the heck is going on?"

Before Jack or Loretta could answer him, Kavi moved closer and said, "Clearly, the time frame has changed since we were airborne. One or another of the national garbage initiatives must have finally taken hold. It is said that before I was born, one plan after another fell to corruption. People were paid off from the top to the bottom, until no money was left to carry out the program. So, when the prime minister announced this recent one during the pandemic, it, too, was considered destined to fail. But, perhaps the pandemic saved it?"

Chris heard this and was interested. "Yeah? How so?"

"People needed work," Kavi replied. "An army of waste-pickers was deputized. A massive, human-powered web was formed to collect and process the garbage." He nodded in the direction of the beachcombers. "Burning was supposed to be curtailed. And it may be that the U.S. inadvertently influenced pollution control, depending on how much time has elapsed between then and ... now. Whenever now might be."

"How's that?"

"Electric vehicles."

I'd heard nothing about this, other than that our government was buying a bunch of them for postal delivery. "Did we donate them?"

"Export them?" Chris added.

Kavi shook his head. "It was simply the example needed. We had ancient cars and trucks that looked to be burning pure coal. But it was the cheaper fuel, not the cleaner, that was the big attraction. We had plenty of electricity, but could not get it where it needed to go. So, maybe the transmission and distribution platforms get a boost in the future." To himself, he said, "If this is true, I might find a position here following my education."

Chris nodded. "An electrical engineer would be super valuable in that case."

Dean grew impatient. "Hello? And why does the garbage and air quality in future-India make any difference to my baseball schedule?"

Everyone ignored him.

Brisa spoke up in a shaky voice. "Jack? Is there some point to all of this that we can take care of so we can go home?" She glanced at me and said tearfully, "All I wanted was to be the assistant director of a college play, and maybe get a little experience with stage makeup."

Jack took pity on her. In that husky voice, she said gently, "Maybe there's a little girl out there, Brisa, someplace in the future, with the same dreams."

B. sniffled. "I suppose that's right. Everyone should be able to—"

"But she *won't* be able to reach for those things if she is sick from bad air."

Loretta, far less gently, put in, "Or if important parts of the food chain die off from choking down your plastic bottles. Or if you people keep arguing about things instead of putting on your big-boy pants and getting to work on them!"

B. burst out crying again, and that hurt me. "Cut it out! It's not *her* fault! If you want to pick on somebody, pick on me. You said this was my job, didn't you?"

"You're not listening," Loretta accused me. "Jack and I said you were a team first; you're just the leader by default." He paused. "Look: now you're arguing about some petty hierarchy when you could just be solving the problem."

"What the hell *is* the problem?" I yelled.

Jack said smoothly, "Why don't you ask Mr. Hamada? He seems to be on the case."

We all pinned our gazes on Chris expectantly.

"What do I know?" he blurted out.

A light came into Kavi's dark eyes. "You're onto the big picture," he said. "Tell you what. Suppose we talk about it over tea?"

***

I had never been to afternoon tea. The Halls were coffee drinkers; so was Brisa's family. I said so, but Kavi told me he'd show us the ropes and that the beverage wasn't as important as the experience.

He started to steer us to a chai cart on one of the immaculate streets near the river, but Jack cut in and said we deserved the full-meal deal. Which, as it turned out, for high tea, meant a lavish spread in the courtyard of the fanciest hotel I'd ever seen.

Until now, that pinnacle had been reached when my grandmother took my parents and me to brunch at the Four Seasons. We'd visited Dad's family fairly regularly when I was little, and that day, Grandma insisted on getting dressed up and going downtown to eat. I hadn't seen her since Grandpa's funeral the previous winter. It had been a day somewhat like the one we'd just left behind at home, in our world—with the promise of spring peeking through cloudy skies. We waltzed into the Four Seasons, checked our coats, and were seated in an opulent dining room lit by chandeliers and scented with delicious aromas. The artful platters of pastries and desserts, plus the steaming plates of Eggs Benedict and smoked meats, held my attention as the grown-ups talked, though I barely touched my food.

When Mom asked me why and encouraged me to take a bite, I had said starkly, "I miss Grandpa." Seeing my grandmother without him there was a first, and rubbed the raw wound in my child's heart.

Grandma looked me in the eye and said solemnly, "We can miss how he was, but we don't have to miss him where we are. He is here."

My response was to cling more tightly. "But ... what happens when *you* die?" I did not want her gone as well. I had never known the set of grandparents on my mother's side.

Grandma chuckled. "No matter what your eyes tell you, Carlita, you can trust what you don't see. The truth is, I'll never die."

I had wanted to believe this, but I'm sure I didn't. In fact, I had never really come around to the idea. Dad had said we had to live for today, "So, eat up!" It was a confusing way to deal with life and death, but a perfect example of how unreconcilable the whole cycle was.

The scene came back to me now as we were seated at a white-clothed table beneath a wide, white tent in the center of an ornamental garden. The five of us, including Kavi, had all goggled at the stately nineteenth-century hotel architecture on the way in. It was a true palace, with three wide, low stories of cream-colored splendor broken by dark, arched windows and breezeways, all capped by little rounded rooftop embellishments, like the tops of acorns spray-painted gold. Even Dean, the European traveler, was rendered speechless.

Brilliant green lawn surrounded the edifice like a sea, visible from the dining tent. "Wow," Chris said as he pulled his chair up to the table. "It's almost as if more space unlocks the mind."

"This is true," Kavi agreed. "The density of the city can be forgotten by the rich—and not-so-rich who visit at tea time. This being my first foray to such a place," he admitted. "How Nanī would exclaim over this. And want me to mind my manners. Pardon, Loretta?" He attempted to contact the director.

"Might I have leave to pop by afterward and tell my esteemed grandparents of our incredible teatime?"

A sound like a live mike being touched was followed by Loretta's voice, somewhat restrained in the fine setting: "That wouldn't be possible, pal. Unless you want to leave your body behind."

"A strange prerequisite..." Kavi murmured.

"Your grandparents won't be here," Jack explained. "At least, not here-now. They would have died many decades in the past."

Now Brisa's eyes widened. "You mean ... this is not now?"

We had all suspected this, but didn't really accept it.

"It's what you'd call the future," Loretta confirmed.

"No me diga," B. exclaimed, floored.

Kavi surveyed the other diners and servers. "But ... it looks the same. I mean, grass is still green and tea is still served at five."

He was right; it didn't look like something out of *Star Trek* or even *Dune*. Male servers were dressed formally, in dark, long coats over tapered pants, while the dining public sported a mix of Western business attire, elegant saris, and colorful headgear. We five surely stuck out in our shorts, jeans, and logo tees, but nobody seemed to notice.

"Humans," Loretta muttered to himself. To Kavi, he said, "To get to the future, people will change much more on the inside than on the outside." He let that sink in. "Now, eat. Drink. *Cīyārsa!*"

***

You know, you only have to time travel once to change on the inside at least a little bit.

If we'd had tea time at the local Denny's—back in there-now, I guess you'd call it—the table chatter would've been the usual: school, sports, music, who was doing what to who. Even if we had somehow taken a field trip to India together and ended up at this palatial garden restaurant, just marveling over the food and different kinds of tea would have been satisfying conversation. But this being here-now, and our unseen directors somehow paying our tab and getting us a ride home, the talk turned to the topic at hand.

Brisa stuffed another round, bite-sized snack into her mouth. "This spicy peanut thing is amazing!" Then she pivoted. "Okay, Carls. Kavi. Hamada. Which one of you has the key to getting us out of here? Not that we have to leave right this second..." She ate another peanut-flavored ball.

Dean set down his delicate china teacup on its matching saucer, both items dwarfed by his pitching hand. "What about me, boss lady?" he demanded of Brisa.

She stopped chewing. "Did you notice how Jack and Loretta want nothing to do with you and me? We are like some kind of science experiment to them. They know we don't have a clue."

Dean couldn't argue with this.

"Those guys, on the other hand—" She took a sip of the orange and cardamom tea that she'd loaded with honey. "—they have at least one miniscule iota of a clue more than we do, so they are the ones being grilled. If you notice. Which you don't."

"You really should pay more attention to your surroundings, big guy," Chris said to Dean with a straight face.

"I'm flattered, B.," I put in, "but I do not have a clue."

Kavi lowered his head and looked at me over his eyeglasses. "Oh, I think you do. But you do not have a clue that you do."

"Whatevs," Brisa said, having regained some composure in the face of free food. "Somebody had better figure out how to get us home before curfew."

"But Jack and Loretta didn't even give us a question this time," I pointed out. "So, I don't know...."

Kavi suggested, "They did give us a hint." At my raised eyebrows, he said, "I believe our journey was the question. What happened first?"

Dean grimaced. "We were out of control and falling."

I pointed at Brisa. "She was screaming her head off..."

"We were flying! Effortlessly!" Chris's enthusiasm washed their negative vibes away. "Over the Earth, halfway around the globe, with a view not even the astronauts ever had! It was so beautiful."

"But then what?" Kavi remained focused.

"It was beautiful until it wasn't," I said slowly, recalling my shock as we got nearer to the ground—the mess, the polluted air, the realization that people were living in there. "I thought the directors were going to dump us in there, but when we landed on the beach, it was all clean."

"All *decades in the future,* you mean," Chris spelled out.

Dean looked back and forth between the two of them. "So?"

Kavi eyed Chris, and then swept a hand at him to take it from there.

"They showed us how things are now. They're showing us how they might be years from now." He set down his teacup with slender fingers that could have been a part of the china set. "They want us to tell them how things need to change in between."

We all looked at each other, saying nothing for a bit, Chris's face bright with expectation. You could feel the respect for a guy who could get the big picture and ask for help moving it out the door.

Kavi muttered to himself, "The sheer scale of an environmental plan this size..."

Brisa wasn't as shabby as she thought she was. "Could get every citizen deputized as a trash-picker. That way, they'd be cleaning up as they go along."

Dean also wanted out of the clueless category. He offered, "Maybe double the amount of recycling centers. However it is they *do* recycling..." he added.

Kavi shook his head. "Not big enough." Quietly, he added, as though piecing it together, "Problems of this size must be handled on a generational level...."

The scent of just-baked scones hit me as the waiter delivered them to our table, and another memory surfaced. I'd had my first scone at the Four Seasons, that day at brunch so long ago. "Guys! I know what it is." As they waited for an answer, my mind drifted inward. I said softly, "Thanks, Grandma."

Chapter 6

My explanation to Jack and Loretta satisfied them, and they returned us to the FCC stage again, much to Brisa's dismay.

"I wanted one more of those peanut things!" she wailed, prompting quizzical looks from Joss and the two actors onstage. We were not about to try to explain our divided loyalties to them. Joss demanded full attention, which was proving to be a problem for her assistant.

Now Malia had lost her focus as Kate. She couldn't find her place on the script and called, "Line!"

But Brisa had lost her focus as AD. When she didn't respond, someone else provided the line asking Cousin Constance whether Mrs. Hardcastle was still trying to hook her up with Tony. As Blaze's Stanzi nodded and wondered why she was considered his perfect match, somebody's phone rang, with a distinctive "La Bamba" tone.

Joss's face clouded over, and she shot a look at her assistant. The bag of devices Brisa had collected when the rehearsal began was stashed in the wings. The sound was coming from B.'s pocket.

I'd rather not relive the next few moments, which were much less pleasant than the smell of the Hooghly River. Let's just say, it was a miracle Brisa escaped with her face intact. But I'll give Joss this: she was efficient. She blew up and dressed down her assistant director in the time it takes to order a coffee from Starbucks, and the rehearsal continued.

This demonstrated the fortitude of the cast. Malia and Blaze went on as though nothing had happened, with Kate explaining to Constance that Mrs. Hardcastle knew her father was dead and her mother wasn't well, and that she would be taking over the family's successful plumbing empire in a year or so. All the better if it were to Tony's—and the Hardcastles'—benefit.

Malia's Kate pointed out her mother's shrewdness: "And this old house just happens to be looking at a complete refit of the pipes—something it'll need if

Moms wants to make a go of the B&B she's got in mind. I'm not surprised to see her trying to snag some free plumbing and marry off Tony at the same time."

Constance wouldn't be dragged into the trap, though. Blaze said, "Who ever thought that Plumber's Crack Incorporated would be a huge romantic draw? But Hastings is my man. I can't bring myself to let your old lady down, though. She's so—rabid. I know I shouldn't, but I let her think I'm in love with her son, and she never dreams that my affections belong to another. Me and Beau are practically living together already."

Kate understood the arrangement. "It works out for Tony too. My good brother is flunking out of senior year again. He wants nothing more than to play video games all day and hit the clubs at night. Women don't seem to enter into the equation, so he's no competition for Beau.... I could almost love him for hating you so much!"

The scene over, Joss called a break. No one dared ask for their phone back to check messages, so cast and crew scattered to the vending machines or the john. Brisa, Dean, Chris, and I fell back, eyeing one another, until Kavi motioned us over to his console in the stage-right wing.

Bathed in the glow of the tiny green light, he looked kind of spooky, with his owlish eyes and dark hair, and his naturally furtive manner. "Quickly! Before they return! I must know, Carli: what did you mean when you said to Jack and Loretta, 'The truth is, I'll never die'? How in the name of Vishnu was that a solution to India's environmental problems? It would seem that would only add to them. I consider myself quite intuitive, and I can recognize the allusion, but I cannot reconcile those words with litter and pollution clean-up." His every nerve seemed to pulsate with anticipation. I didn't know how he'd held off asking until the end of the scene.

A smile played over my lips as I thought back to thinking back. "It was a quote from my grandma. She said it to me to let me know she'd always be with me. But what I meant by it was, persuade everyone that cleaning up the environment will make life better for those who come after them."

I watched his reaction. It was like the sun coming up over the Bay of Bengal. "Because of the belief in *punarjanma!*" he exclaimed, his whole body shaking.

Giving me this much credit was a little embarrassing, to be honest. Anyone could tell that Kavi was light-years ahead of me or the rest of us intellectually. "It was nothing," I mumbled. Then I cracked a grin. "But it *was* pretty spot on, huh?"

Chris was right there with us. "A people who believe in reincarnation would be predisposed to acting on behalf of the next generation, or the next incarnation, or something." He held out a fist to bump. "Good one, Carli. Today, India—tomorrow the world!"

Brisa envied me the attention, but she graciously seconded Chris's fist bump. Even Dean seemed to appreciate my insight, yet he sensed its limits. "That might work with people who believe they'll come back as birds or whatever," he said thoughtfully. "But what good would that do us in this country? Americans care about the here and now."

Brisa's eyes narrowed. "The way some people just love to make laws protecting babies all the way up until birth, but the second you're born, you're on your own."

"Fetuses," Chris corrected her. "They're not babies until they're born."

"And that's when they really need help. As soon as you breathe air, somebody out there can't wait to take it away from you."

"Really?" I said. "There are crooks outside the maternity ward just waiting to stick up babies and steal their pacifiers?"

"Well, they say there's a sucker born every minute," Chris quipped. "I guess that's what that means."

"Speaking of which..." Dean drew our attention to the approach of Dave B. and Mason. "Here are two right now."

This reminded me that Dean Dixon was part of the sporting group, and that we weren't the same breed. It might be wise not to get too friendly with this dog.

***

The two actors made ready for their scene, as Spider Marlow and Beau Hastings arrive at the Hardcastle house, believing it to be a functioning inn owned by Tony's father. Having just met Tony at the pub, they are unknowingly the butt of his joke: He offers them a place to stay the night, but they don't realize that he is the brother of Spider's blind date, Kate ... or that Kate's cousin, Constance—who is Beau's "boo"—is staying there while her mother is hospitalized. So, they wander in, already completely wrong about everything.

One of the servants, tray in hand, ushers them into the drawing room. "Welcome! Our first customers. This way."

Dave B.'s exaggerated style was just right for Hastings, and he had already memorized his lines. He began, "After the overbookings of the day, welcome once more, Spider, to the comforts of a clean room and a tray of..." He pretended to peer at the servant's offering. "Gummi Bears." He paused a beat, then breezed on. "It was cool of Tony to offer to let us sleep on his couch, but it looks like there are plenty of rooms in this mausoleum. Word: not a bad house ... antique, but it's got four walls and a roof."

Mason's Marlow sounded like a know-it-all, but he did have to glance at his script first: "The usual fate of a large mansion. Once the kids have moved away, their rooms are turned into a poor-man's vacation rental."

Dave's Hastings expected better: "And here we are to help pay off the second mortgage and the property tax. The days of cheap online rentals are over. They lure you in with a plate of free Gummi Bears—" He pretended to take one from the tray and chew it. "—but then they nickel and dime you for the mini-bar."

Marlow commiserated, "Nomads on spring break, Beau-Man, must pay what the market will bear. But at least there are Gummi Bears!" He addressed the servant. "Are these the CBD kind?"

The servant boy shook his head.

Hastings, Marlow's college roommate, continued, "You live the dream, my friend. Every break you're in Aspen, Cancun, Fort Lauderdale. I'd think that you, who have seen so much of the world, would have a better ... *feel* for the ladies. You may be able to handle texting, but remember, bro: you can't have sex remotely."

Marlow frowned. "I blame the pandemic. It's been murder on my self-esteem. My life has become one long Zoom class, in seclusion from that lovely part of creation that gives men a reason to build confidence. It's been years since I've met a single modest woman—except my mother, of course. But among females of another class..."

Hastings nodded. "...all bets are off. I know. I've seen you in action. But in the company of women who are smarter or hotter than you, I never saw such an idiot."

They go on to recall how Spider is all that on the phone, but in person, he can't pull it off. Coffee dates and chick flicks and mutual consent? Way too much stress. So, Beau asks him how he'll make it through the blind date that is the reason they wound up at Tony's place.

Marlow plans to go through the motions, but that's about it. "Actually, Beau-Man," he said, "I only agreed to come along to be *your* wingman, not the other way around. Connie Neville digs you, the family don't know you, and as my friend, you'll already be seen as golden."

This brings up a possible ulterior motive. "Good old Marlow!" Beau said, and paused. "You do know I'm not after her money, though. Right? Miss Neville's bod is all I ask; now all I have to do is steal that away from her controlling auntie, who has charge of both that and her bank account."

Just then, Mr. Hardcastle enters to interrupt them. But first Joss had to nudge Brisa, who had to yell at Dean to take his cue.

Watching the three of them, I got that yearning feeling Joss had been talking about. Mason as Marlow, with his ease and something about his strong, tanned fingers holding his script, made me wish once more that I'd been cast opposite him, as Kate, so I'd have an excuse to eyeball him. Dave B. played Hastings with irony and good timing, not to mention all of his speech delivered by heart. It was just great acting, but he couldn't be a greater foil for Dean's Mr. Hardcastle. In a way, I could see why Joss had given Dean the blockhead role, but in another way, I couldn't believe that she thought he could act. He could read, and words rolled off his tongue, but his emotion was all wrong, i.e., nonexistent. I yearned for a better Mister for my Missus.

But it was early days yet in the production. He might improve.... Ah, who was I kidding? I alternated between wanting to cheer and wanting to shrivel up throughout their scene.

Dean read from his script, his rich radio voice never once conveying the correct tone for Hardcastle. "'Gentlemen, once more you are heartily welcome. Which is Mr. Marlow?'"

Mason, on the other hand, *was* Marlow. "Call me Spider."

"'Mr., er, Spider, I regret that I was not at hand to receive you at the gate. You are earlier than expected. I'd like to have provided a hearty reception and see that your horses and trunks were taken care of.'"

Marlow rolled his eyes at Hastings. "He has got our names from the Internet already." To Hardcastle, he replied, "Well, we came in his Tesla, and we're traveling light. Just these messenger bags. Change of underwear and some things for the ladies." He turned toward Hastings and pantomimed pulling open his shirt to expose his chest. "They do love a man who pretends to be a feminist. But this one may be old-school. Do you think I should hide my 'Votes for Women' tattoo?"

Hardcastle, who knows Spider is to be Kate's date, insists he not stand on ceremony in his house. "'This is a free country, gentlemen,'" Dean read. "'You may do just as you please here.'"

Marlow sighed. "Well, that's a relief!" Mason pulled a real beer can from a pocket and pretended to crack it open and drain half of it. This reminded me how valuable a prop can be.

Hardcastle: "'Your love of ale and the ladies, Mr. Marlow, puts me in mind of my days sowing my wild oats. Why, I remember when—'"

Mason's Marlow drained his can and said to Hastings: "Looks like we're going to need a beer run."

Dean's Hardcastle rambled on, "'—once drank the better part of a keg of nut-brown and then went a-calling—'"

Dave B.'s Hastings, ignoring him, said, "You go, then, Spide. I'm not sure I can take another welcome by this guy."

Hardcastle tried to get their attention. "'I say, gentlemen, as I was telling you, we drank so much that the ladies then had to provide mop and bucket—'"

Marlow continued, "Well, I'm not going, Beau-Man. I've got a blind date. Our friend fixed me up with his sister. Maybe she knows someone for you."

Here, the audience knows that she knows someone, and who that someone is.

But Hardcastle went on, "'—knee-deep in vomit, and we—'"

To shut him up, Marlow said, "What if, my good man, you gave us a glass of punch in the meantime; it would help us loosen up for the ladies."

Hardcastle was supposed to be outraged at the rude request, but Dean didn't get it. He read the line like a demand: "Punch, sir!"

Even Joss couldn't take it. "Dixon! It sounds like you're asking him to punch you." She demonstrated the outrage. "It's, '*Punch,* sir?' As in, *how dare you?*"

Dean copied her, barely, then continued reading, "'This is the most unaccountable kind of modesty I ever met with. Most unlike his father.'"

Marlow: "Yes, sir, 'punch.' You know, some hard cider. A cocktail. Better yet, a six pack. This is a free country, you know. *Choice* is the watchword."

Dean did pretend to rummage around in an imaginary cooler, then acquiesced, "'I believe I have a couple of Budweiser Zeroes, men. Your choice—this one, or this one."

Marlow, skeptically: "So, a one-time party animal now drinks near-beer. Well, it's better than nothing."

Hastings, ruefully: "No, it's not."

Marlow then trolled Hardcastle, "From the excellence of your cellar, my friend, I suppose you have tons of business these days. Travelers can be demanding."

And, of course, Hardcastle didn't get it. "'No, sir, truly, you are our first customers. Tell no one, but we have yet to gain the business permit needed for us that sell ale.'" Dean gave a blatant, open-mouthed wink.

Hastings was beginning to suspect he was being used. "No hotel permit or liquor license? So, then, you have no friends in politics, right?"

Hardcastle walked right into the trap. "'Only Mr. Marlow's esteemed father.'"

Hastings eyed Marlow. "Strange coincidence... Maybe Spider here can put in a good word for you, Hardcastle.

Hardcastle: "'A good word? Well, that was the expectation....'"

Now it was Marlow's turn to be offended. "What an arrogant bastard. But, hey, who needs a hotel permit when you have such a forceful argument in your cup, old man." He raised the beer can.

Hardcastle: "'Breakfast of champions, as you young people say.'"

Brisa cut in, calling, "Exit Marlow and Hardcastle!"

Mason and Dean trooped offstage.

Hastings, alone now, turned to the audience and said, "So far, I give this place two stars. But there's

still time for 'the help' to improve my final Trip
Investigator review."

Dave B. bowed low, and everyone broke into
applause for the laugh line.

***

Other than Dean's amateurish efforts, I did like
how the play was shaping up. Practicing in stages,
we had finished Act One and would be through
Act Two next week. Meanwhile—ugh—Dean and I
had a standing date to run lines on Tuesdays before
rehearsal. I was having to kick my butt to get my
homework done the rest of the time.

So, I wasn't too surprised to see my Contemporary
Issues paper zitted with red marks when Mr. Pentek
handed them back to the class on Monday morning.
The topic had been "The Next Pandemic," and we
were supposed to choose a recent covid-19 issue and
apply it to how we should deal with the next public
health emergency. In a two-page paper, I saw the
notation sources??? half a dozen times.

"I've *got* sources," I grumbled to myself, but the next
second I knew I'd been lazy. Pentek told us to back
up our claims with references, so I had looked over

my paper's assertions—that masks were effective virus deterrents, that online learning had certain consequences—and then worked backwards. It took just a few minutes of Googling to find a couple of websites that supported what I'd said.

Pentek was onto me, and I wasn't alone in my tactic.

Our civics teacher was a wiry man, not too tall, with short, neatly cut blackish hair that had some drifts of snow at his ears. He was sharp but fair, with an "always on" type of energy. You could see that the school district got back every penny they shelled out for him, and then some. Maybe he was paid by the red mark, I thought, sliding my embarrassment of a paper underneath my open notebook.

Today, Pentek wasn't buying the mistakes we'd made in presenting our analyses of our research and opinions. He remarked that no one had done better than a B minus on these papers, which showed we needed a refresher on fake news. "If you start out from a faulty factual point," he said, pacing the front of the room like a cat in the zoo, "your opinions will suck. And that's a fact." He grinned and sat down on the edge of his desk, adding, more seriously, "You may also make bad decisions based on crap information. There are plenty of people and companies and websites that want you to do that— some to make money, others just to put one over on you. And you don't want to be the one who got fooled twice."

Everyone winced.

This put me in mind of the play. Tony fools Mrs. Hardcastle into thinking he has romantic designs on Constance Neville, and he fools Hastings and Marlow into thinking they are at some obscure B&B instead of the home of Marlow's actual date, Kate. Marlow doesn't yet know he's been set up with her by his own father and Mr. Hardcastle; instead, he thinks Tony has done him a solid by getting him some female company for the night.

Already, I thought, everyone is acting on faulty factual points—except for Tony, who doesn't give a damn, as long as someone else keeps Miss Neville busy so he can go out drinking with his friends. And that was just the beginning of the night's mistakes. Pentek was right; starting from the wrong point could lead to a cascade of wrong decisions. Like the one I'd made in choosing my references for this paper. I drew a wiggly line at the top of my notebook with an arrow at one end pointing one way and another arrow at the other end pointing the other way.

Then a guy sitting across the aisle, who I considered to be at least as smart as me, raised his hand with a troubled expression. "Mr. Pentek! I gave two sources for everything I said was true, but you still marked me down for them. What's up?"

Our teacher didn't even have to look at the offending paper to answer the question. "Yours was the same problem as everyone else who got dinged for those, Mr. Dulinger. Yes, I did make two Web references the minimum requirement, per claim. But websites like SoCrazyItsTrue and TheDailyKlingon are not the best places to get important facts. It's not just the number of citations, it's the quality of your sources that gives your ideas their integrity."

In my notebook, I wrote down the names of those websites, so I could type them into my phone later and see if they were real or not.

Someone else called out, "What if you've got no sources but buckets of original ideas that are really great?"

Dulinger replied, "You've still got to show why they hold water."

Pentek leaned forward. "That's right. And how do we do that?" He didn't wait for a show of hands. "By getting corroboration. In other words, somebody *else* who is trustworthy thinks those ideas are sound. The same with references. Now, let's go over how we locate these trustworthy sources again."

He didn't sound exasperated, even though we had learned how to vet news-and-views sources at the beginning of the semester. I recalled now some of the criteria we were supposed to look for: who funds the site; whether we automatically agree or disagree without reading anything first; and what other reputable sources have to say about that site. I knew I hadn't done any of those things, just decided what I wanted to hear and then searched for it online. I didn't mind Mr. Pentek reviewing the right way to do things, since I might have to apply those standards to one of Brisa's tall tales someday. I grinned to myself.

"These pesky steps are hard to take sometimes," Pentek admitted, "even for me. We all have built-in biases about what we think should be the truth, and we all want to be right." He went to the whiteboard and wrote, cherry-picking. "Everybody has done this. We choose the news sources or just snippets of information that repeat what we want to be true or what we believe to be true—whether it is or not. So, objectivity and context matter."

I drew a picture of a cherry tree in my civics notebook. Maybe I shouldn't have written that stuff about remote learning not working and setting kids' education back by years. That could be true in some cases but not in others. Like, Mom was having me take a safe-driving course online to get a better insurance rate. I complied so I could drive every now and then, and maybe get my own car before I turned a hundred years old. After going through driver's ed in person, the computer course was a breeze.

When Mr. Pentek asked for examples of how cherry-picking could make you look right when you might be wrong or just not totally right, I offered my own paper as evidence and told them about the online course.

"Yes!" he replied, pointing at me. "And it could be that, by accident, you do cherry-pick from the correct sources. But you want to get lots of practice in vetting where you get your information before you cut corners like that."

This sounded fair. And it would've helped the players in *Mistakes of a Night* avoid at least some of their mistakes. Tony Lumpkin was obviously not the most truthful source.

Now to figure out how to tell Mom why I got a C on my class paper ... right after I looked up TheDailyKlingon to see whose money was behind it.

Chapter 7

P lay practice the next day went like clockwork—
that is, in here-now time, in which one
moment is followed by a sequential moment in the
same place. Lines were supposed to be delivered by
heart, and for the most part, they were. Given Dean's
limited attention span, we had committed only the
dialogue that would be used right away to memory.
Then we'd repeat the previous passages over again
with each new chunk that he learned.

Meanwhile, I was doing all this at home, by myself,
and at lunchtimes, with Brisa's help. We were pretty
good at ignoring the *you-kook* looks from our fellow
diners as we recited the play with gusto. B. enjoyed
doing her impressions of each actor impersonating
their characters. But, as it turned out, she did not
enjoy someone doing an impression of her.

In our reading later that week, Mrs. Hardcastle
is flirting with Beau Hastings and asks what he

thinks of her fancy new facemask. Brisa's Hastings, which was even bigger than Dave B.'s Hastings, said as an aside, "The height of fashion—not!" Then to Mrs. H., Brisa attempted Beau's false flattery, but struggled with the French: "Extremely elegant and ... *dega- dega-gee*, upon my word, madam. Is it a Chanel?" She pronounced it "channel."

I snorted, and thought I was following B.'s lead by ad-libbing, in a Spanglish accent, *"¡Dios mío, ayúdame!* We can't all *eh*-speak perfect French like the Mexicans." Then I busted out laughing, drawing stares from nearby cafeteria tables.

Brisa snapped her eyes open and shut. "Ex-squeeze me? Did I say something wrong?"

After taking a breath, I managed, "It's *dégagée. Dégagée,*" I repeated in a sexy French accent. "And it's Cha-*nel,* not like a TV channel." I paused. "Channel Number Five!" This grabbed my funny bone, for some reason, and I tumbled into another wave of laughter.

That only deepened Brisa's frown and mood. "Since when do the Cubans know so much about French?" she demanded.

Frankly, this Cuban American didn't. I had just heard Dave B. practicing with his reflection in a window before rehearsal. I mean, I'd heard the word *degagée* before, but I had no idea that's how you spelled it until I saw it in the script just now. As for Chanel, we all knew of the designer and the perfume. Maybe Brisa hadn't been expecting it to come up.

Now I realized I'd kind of embarrassed her, but I didn't want to let on. "We Cubans can't help it if we're better educated," I razzed her.

"Is-that-what-you-think-of-us?" she snapped at Outrage Level 10, which was tempered by Butt-Hurt Level 5, leaving the phrase to weakly sail off into the industrial lunch–smelling atmosphere.

"Test scores don't lie," I said with my chin raised, referring to the disparity in our SAT results, which we'd both received the previous week. Actually, she'd done a hair better in math than me, but I'd smoked her on the verbal, possibly because her family read and wrote in Spanish more often than mine.

She could've argued with me over her math score and Spanish fluency, but instead she said nothing, checking the wall clock and then mumbling something about getting to gym class. I should've known this would not just blow over. When Brisa got quiet, it was just the calm before the storm.

***

Perhaps by accident, Dean showed up at the theater on time, right at five. Again, I had rushed home from school, crammed in my chores and a bowl of cereal, and rushed over to the community college. I saw one of the double doors swing open and a rectangle of light propel Dean from the hallway to the ramp down toward the stage, his voluminous white shorts wafting around his legs like a robe, as though he were Jesus in some Hollywood dolly shot.

I didn't want him to think I held him sacred. Jumping into Mrs. Hardcastle's role, I ad-libbed, "Clever of this rogue to disguise himself in the athletic shorts of Jesus Christ." Then I knelt down onstage and quoted from the script, "Take pity on us, good Mr. Highwayman! Take our money, our watches, all we have, but spare our lives!"

Dean pointed a toe in its size-12 Nike and twisted a leg this way and that. "These legs do look rather celestial, don't they?"

"More like *hell*-estial, if you ask me." Now I pretended to be a beauty-queen judge. "I give 'em a five out of ten."

He looked hurt. "Really?"

And I just had to be tough. "Really." I turned and headed for the stage-right wing, pretending that I had something to ask Kavi. "Be right back."

For no good reason, I kept him waiting. When I returned, he was sitting on a folding chair like *The Thinker,* only with both fists holding up his chin. Someone had written in marker on his knuckles p-i-o-n on one hand, and e-e-r-s on the other. From a distance, it looked like a cheat sheet. I joked, pointing to his team slogan and warning, "Joss will notice if you write your lines on the back of your hands, dude."

Again, hurt glinted in his eyes before he glossed it over by sticking his fists out. "Pioneers, number one! Where's your school spirit, huh?"

And then he surprised me by wading right in with the answering riposte to my highwayman parry. As Mr. Hardcastle, Dean said, "I believe the woman's out of her senses. What, Dorothy, don't you know *me?*" And he even put the emphasis where it was supposed to go.

I was speechless for a moment, then, wracking my brain for the rest of the scene, I sputtered, letting the Missus babble. "Mr. Hardcastle, as I'm alive!" I put a hand to my forehead. "My fears blinded me. But who, my dear, could have expected to meet you here, in this frightful place, so far from home? What has brought you to follow us?"

Before he could reply, a voice from the center ramp, out in the dim recess of theater seats, called, "It is I, Chris Hamada, bearing gifts for two needy actors."

I fell out of character. "What's that?" I asked, as Chris emerged into the glow from the stage.

"Talent," he said, miming as if to toss some our way. Dean's reflexes kicked in—either the sports ones or the acting ones—and he fake-caught the bundle of talent.

Maybe due to guilt over my earlier faux pas with Brisa, I took this the wrong way. "Up yours, Hamada."

"Up his what?" Kavi asked, strolling from between the wing curtains.

"My very big brain, Mr. Das," Chris said to him, reaching over and getting the surprised engineer in a cartoon headlock.

I suddenly wanted out of here, but in the conventional manner, of my own accord. "Don't look now, *amigos,* but here comes our assistant director, by coincidence." Brisa was making her way down the ramp, followed by two of the college crew members. I wondered if she was speaking to me. I addressed the group ominously, "This puts us, the Hot Five, in the spotlight, and you know what that means."

Chris said, "I can't wait!" and at the same time, Dean grumbled, "I'm not in the mood for Loretta today."

Brisa walked up to him and linked her arm through his. "Let's run away together then," she suggested, ignoring me.

"Let's try to avoid that," I countered. "I'd love to just stay here and have a nice, quiet rehearsal. In the here-now. Or is it the now-here?" I cocked my head at Chris, but he walked off with Kavi, and Brisa followed them. So, I was left to finish my recital with Dean until the rest of the cast arrived.

Joss had Dean and Mason reprise their last Hardcastle and Marlow scene, with Dave B. coming in as Hastings and Blaze as Miss Neville. The rest of us weren't onstage today, but we five were following along uneasily. It was hard to keep my whole attention on the action while waiting for our next command performance.

But it never came. We finished the scenes, Joss gave us her notes, and Dean offered to drive us home.

Brisa again sat up front with him, and the atmosphere in the jeep was a mixture of friction and relief. "Well, guys," Dean said as he pulled out of the community college parking lot onto the main street. "We managed to control our own destinies tonight. What's up with that?"

"Maybe *los directores* decided we're more trouble than we're worth," Brisa supposed.

"Maybe they finished what they started," I said hopefully.

Kavi nixed that idea from beside me in the backseat. "This is out of character for those two. They clearly had an agenda, and that agenda could not yet have been successfully fulfilled. They have not, for example, polled each of us for our priorities or our solutions."

"I'm ready anytime," Chris said, sounding disappointed that the rehearsal had ended without our being summoned by Jack and Loretta. "Those of us with *real talent* should be prepared to extemporize." He leaned across Kavi to make sure the inference was not lost on me.

It wasn't lost on Brisa, either. "Yeah, Carli. Real talent," she said pointedly. "Maybe, someday, someone will make you AD. As they say, those who can, direct. Those who can't, just act."

***

Despite the veiled bickering, we agreed to all go out together after practice on Friday night. The Hot Five needed some fun. There was a sports bar near the college that let minors in before nine. If we got out of rehearsal on time, that'd give us long enough to eat and play a couple of video games.

But when I got home, Mom informed me that I would not be doing that.

My mother, Reza Hall, was a pretty good-looking forty-one, I had to admit, which had made it easy for her to get back into the dating scene after divorcing Dad. She dyed any portion of her chin-length, layered hair that was not absolutely jet-black, and she used sunscreen like plaster, so she looked a good ten years younger than she really was. She also worked out with hand weights, so that her upper arms did not have that bird-wing look that happens when women age, and she did Jazzercise so she'd be fit enough for her outdoor job, messing around lakes and wells and pipes and stuff, collecting samples for water testing. The upshot was a mother who gave her teenage daughter a run for her money.

She was totally chill about it, though, so I could not begrudge her a great reflection in the mirror. She didn't bug me about my appearance, either. But she did bug me about my grades.

As we sat at the round kitchen table eating chocolate ice cream out of coffee mugs, she asked me to explain my civics paper grade. As if in solidarity, Teddy Roosevelt, lying under the table hoping we'd drop some ice cream in his mouth, gave a lazy whine. I had strategically left my paper on the kitchen counter late the night before and slipped out the door a tad early this morning. It did buy me some time.

But what good was time, really?

Mom set down her spoon. "Carli, a C is not like you. Is the play cutting into your studies?"

The possible loss of the third-most crucial thing I had ever wanted knifed through me. The lesser role of Mrs. Hardcastle had taken its place in my mental hierarchy, right after the second-most crucial thing (Kate) that I didn't get but now wasn't sure that I'd ever needed. "No, no! Rehearsals are only two days a week. I got tripped up by this 'news literacy' thing in Mr. Pentek's class. You know, how to spot fake news? And how to use real news. It's ... tricky."

I didn't bother telling her that nobody else got above a B minus. That never worked to get any sympathy. Mom wasn't going to change her mind about Friday night, but she was impressed that I'd used my safe-driving course as an example to show the class why the premise of my paper was wrong. She'd way rather hear me admit to being wrong than trying to convince her I was right.

Which was why I had to mislead her a little bit when she brought up my role in *Mistakes of a Night*.

"I think you were brave to stick with it when your plans changed, *mi querida*. I'm so sorry you didn't get to play the lead like you wanted."

"Turns out, maybe I wanted the wrong thing without knowing it. I like being Mrs. Hardcastle, and I've got this crotchety, snooty voice I use that Joss loves."

"So, a happy accident," Mom said, spooning up some melted ice cream and clinking her spoon into the mug. Teddy, giving up, got to his feet and padded out of the kitchen. "Sounds like it's all going along just fine," Mom concluded. When I didn't respond, she looked at me and double-checked, "Is it?"

Unless I wanted to open the floodgates of maternal investigation into my mental health, I could not tell her about the two ... incidents. Or that we had expected another incident today that didn't happen. Or that the architects of these other-worldly episodes were invisible creatures who held our group of five friends in contempt, as well as in service to some unknown agenda that may or may not be constructive. I also could not bring up the callous way I'd treated my best friend, even though it was just a little thing; Mom had considered Brisa and me joined at the hip since third grade. And I didn't want her to think poorly of Chris, who had probably just been joking about my acting skill level.... Right?

So, I nodded and dropped my spoon in my empty coffee mug and gave her just a tiny bit of fake news. "Going along just fine, Mom."

Chapter 8

That night, I dreamed I was flying over an unfamiliar, exotic landscape with Teddy Roosevelt beside me, his ears blown back and tongue out. That dog loved a good adventure.

His greatest real-life achievement to date had been summiting one of the lower mountaintops in the national forest. I kept the framed photo of him, with an expression much the same as the one in my dream, on the magnetic board in my bedroom. Paws atop a boulder, the majesty of the mountain range and blue sky as his backdrop, my black Lab literally stood on top of the world.

As I lay there in bed peeking at his picture across the room, the real Teddy had muscled his way inside, hitting the door with a meaty shoulder and activating the loose latch. I rubbed his soft ears as he snuffled the bedclothes.

"I wish I could take you with me next time," I told him, assuming there would be a next-time incident with Jack and Loretta.

The photo was proof that Teddy had once accompanied Mom on one of her periodic solo trips, backpacking in the wilderness area of the nearby national forest. Every now and then, she'd get a wild hair and tell Dad and me to drop her off at a trailhead, with a pickup rendezvous time. That had been the only weeklong woman-dog backpacking trip, though. Teddy had been great about carrying his own food and gear in a doggy pack. But Mom said she wasn't so keen on stopping to bury his poops, as leave-no-trace protocol demanded. It wasn't the grossness factor, she said, so much as the look on his face as he watched her put his poop where a bone should have been.

He did have one soulful face.

I thought of it with longing now, as I lay in the dark, cold, and damp, in a hollow carved out of forest hillside. The night seemed endless and silent, until I focused on the tiniest of scratching, scraping sounds in the dirt around me. I wasn't alone. But I sure wished Teddy were here.

I did feel alone, despite the creepy crawlers, as the Hot Five faction had devolved to five individuals, some of whom professed hatred of me and others that I didn't feel I could trust with my life. And that was the gist of the most recent Jack-and-Loretta challenge: how to get anywhere safely in a strange location, far from the comforts of home, with five people who couldn't or wouldn't agree.

And not twenty-four hours earlier, we'd been having one of our best and funniest rehearsals to date. We had doubled back to the scene where Mr. Hardcastle and Marlow exit to look for snacks to go with the beer, leaving Beau Hastings alone in the drawing room—where Constance finds him. Dave B.'s Hastings and Blaze's Constance were poised to discover their first mistake of the night.

Brisa announced the scene. "Battle of the blonds: you're on!"

Dave B. was in a rare mood tonight. He feigned happy surprise at the sight of his boo, and channeled a horny Hastings hopped up on Green Bull: "Wait— what? *Another* coincidence?" he exclaimed, with far more shock than necessary. "Miss Neville, in the house!"

Blaze decided to play the forward schoolgirl. She leapt across the stage, blonde ponytail and short skirt flying, and embraced Dave B. like he was wearing a Velcro suit. "Babe!" her Constance yipped. "To what unexpected good fortune am I to ascribe this happy meeting?"

Hastings struggled to escape her grip, twisting and turning until he pulled free. "Twist of fate, maybe? Save it for the bedroom, sweetheart. I should ask you: what are you doing at this second-rate Internet inn?"

She wasn't sure what he was talking about. "Internet inn! You must be mistaken: my aunt, my guardian, lives here. What makes you think this house is an inn?" She sidled up close to him again.

He backed away. "My friend Spider Marlow and I are on spring break, and everything was booked up. We were sent here by a guy we met at the Naked Parrot. Nice fellow."

"OMG, it must be one of my hopeful cousin's tricks!" Constance advanced on him again, grabbing his hand and pulling him down to sit beside her where two folding chairs had been placed to act as a couch. "You've heard me bitch about Tony a million times, haven't you?"

The truth dawned on Hastings. "*That* Tony? The one your aunt wants to fix you up with? My main competition?"

She nodded. "You have nothing to fear from him, Babylove. You'd adore him, if you knew how much he despises me. My aunt, however, thinks she's getting somewhere, so I let her think so. Keeps her off my back, which she basically owns until I turn twenty-one and inherit the family business."

"My dear dissembler!" Dave B. leaned over and caressed Blaze's cheek. "You must know, Stanzi, I have been making plans for our getaway to a more liberal state—one where we might still retain the right to vote and live a child-free life, if we so choose."

Blaze jumped up. "I've told you, Beau, that I'll follow you to the ends of the state line, but still ... I'm not sure I'm ready to give up my little fortune. I have no brothers, and Daddy always wanted me to carry on with the family's plumbing empire." She sniffled and shed a melodramatic tear. "I've held off on going to college, knowing that I'll always have a trade."

Someone offstage called out, "She's got a trade! The world's oldest profession!"

Everybody cracked up, and Blaze struck a streetwalker pose, her prim ponytail and uniform skirt adding a touch of irony. "Does that make you my pimp?" she asked Dave B. "Or my john?"

Joss held her hands up until people stopped laughing, and nodded to Brisa.

"Places!" B. barked. "Take it from 'I'll always have a trade.'" And more snickers followed, but Brisa turned and snarled for quiet.

Ever the professional, Blaze faded back into character. "Daddy always wanted me to carry on with the family's plumbing empire," she repeated, trying to keep a straight face. "The instant they hand me the golden wrench, I'll be ready to run away with you, Beau, and open a new Plumber's Crack in whichever state will have us." She struggled to maintain composure as the guffaws rose.

Dave B. articulated in rapid fire over the noise, "Why wait? Your person is all! I! desire! I'm graduating in two months. And my BA in English should get me steady work at a Coffeebucks! Just think about it, sweetums." Then he suggested he and Constance perpetuate the ruse. "In the meantime, let's not tell Marlow that Tony and the Naked Parrot gang are probably still laughing about this. He's got a blind date, and I don't want him to up and leave before he finds out who it is."

"But it must be with Kate!" Constance presumed. "And Tony thought he'd throw a monkey wrench in the works. He doesn't want his old man to rent out his room. But how will we keep Spider in the dark?"

"Enter, Marlow!" bellowed Brisa as Mason crossed the stage, followed by one of Kavi's spots.

"What's that?" Marlow said. "In the dark? It can't get any darker than this. Our host could spring for another light bulb or two." Mason rubbed his eyes. "What have we got here?"

"My-dear-Spider!" Hastings greeted him too forcefully. "The most fortunate accident! Who do you think just happens to be staying here?"

Spider was not the least bit curious. "Cannot guess."

Hastings continued, with way too much enthusiasm, "Our double dates, dog, Miss Hardcastle and Miss Neville! You've met Stanzi, here, and as it turns out, the innkeeper's daughter, Kate, is your blind date. She'll be back in a minute!"

"Oh, shit. The old-school babe." Marlow regarded his visible chest tattoo and ripped jeans. "And me, with nothing to change into." He moved to Hastings and gripped his shoulder. "Beau-man, you must not go. You are to assist me. I always say the wrong thing."

Hastings brushed away his hand. "Got to go! Sometimes a wingman's gotta fly. She's just a woman, you know."

Blaze took this opportunity to put hands on hips and glare Constance's ire at him.

Not noticing, Marlow said, "That's the problem. She's a woman. What I need is a wench. Them, I can talk to."

Again, someone called from offstage, "You can take your pick from the crew!"

A crew member squealed, and sounds of a mock tussle ensued.

This was entertaining, but almost as good was Joss's attempt to restore order. With everyone now in an uproar, she reached backstage to where the fire extinguisher and emergency supplies hung on the wall, and let loose a blast from an airhorn.

That did it.

As the ringing in my ears subsided, though, I heard neither our director's voice nor Mason's Spider impression. The stage went dark and silent, and the electronic sound of a hand touching a microphone gave two puffy beats.

"Is this thing on?" came a sultry voice.

And that was the last time I saw the theater, as I knew it, for quite some time.

***

The two directors—neither of them Joss Morales, by the way—had once more isolated the five of us from the assembled cast and crew, and started chatting away, as though we—and they—had nothing better to do.

"What a week," Jack began. "If it wasn't one thing on the far side of the galaxy, it was another."

"And the emails!" Loretta complained. "You should see our inbox. Past generations, future generations ... losers like you. Everybody wanting to know something."

Kavi inquired from his darkened console, "You still use emails?"

"What *you'd* think of as emails," Loretta said condescendingly. "What they really are, are—" He rattled off some combination of letters, numbers, grunts, and clicks, finishing it off with, "and the home of the brave!"

No one knew how to respond. Then Brisa, somewhere near me, said, "Yeah, well, you just hit Reply, stick in a few emojis, and you're done. Unless yours doesn't work as good as ours."

Jack chuckled. "Oh, we've got super high-speed Xkt56d_3gh *ugh, tch! tch!* and the home of the brave. We've just had so many inquiries, we've been swamped. Sorry we missed you on Tuesday."

"Don't be," shot back Dean. "We had a great time without you."

Somewhere in the darkness, Chris stepped in. "Ah, don't listen to him. We were wondering where you were. Life is so dull when you don't show up and complicate things beyond belief."

"Boo-hoo," Loretta retorted. "Sucks when things get complicated, huh?"

"No," Chris said sincerely. "I love it."

Forgetting I was pissed at him, I affirmed, "He does."

Jack said to me, "But you don't love it when he calls you a no-talent wannabe."

"Hey!" Chris broke in. "I never—"

My stomach got that accordion feeling again as I relived the moment when he might as well have called me that.

"And Brisa," Jack continued, "doesn't love it when those who are not of Mexican extraction make sweeping generalizations about the Mexican people as a group, even in jest."

A bit of silence ensued as the others probably wondered what she was talking about. Meanwhile, I went deep into the Land of Shame, and Brisa probably said to herself, *You're damn right!*

Right over the Land of Shame sailed a cloud of Freaky Weird Apprehension as I wondered how the hell they knew what we'd been doing and even, I guessed, the thoughts in our heads. I wrestled with this for a moment, coming up with no possible answers. As I was about to put a question into words, though, Loretta cut me off.

"Hold that thought. Stick it in an email, babe, and we'll get to it."

Dean, off toward the stage-right wing, cleared his throat. "You're busy, we're busy. Why don't we just call it a night? We've got places to go."

"Why, yes," Jack agreed unctuously. "You do."

He groaned.

I spoke up. "Okay. We do have to get back to rehearsal. What do you want from me this time?"

"Not you," Loretta said. "Science experiments! Front and center. Thing 1!"

Brisa said slowly, "You mean..."

Dean cleared his throat again. "And I'm..."

"That's right. Thing 2! I've got the original question for the both of you. What do you consider the biggest problem facing mankind?"

They didn't respond.

Loretta popped a cork. "Chop-chop! You want to go back to your sad, little lives? Let's get on with it!"

Trying to smooth things over, Jack repeated the question in a more reasonable tone.

"You know what I think?" Brisa ventured. "I think it's crime. There's always somebody out there who can't wait to take away—"

"Yeah, yeah, your stuff," Loretta finished. "Crime. Biggest problem in the world. People wanting stuff, getting stuff, and taking stuff. Never mind they might be taking it because they need it. But, sure. Let's say it's crime."

"And you, Thing 2," Jack said to Dean, causing Chris and me to giggle, even in our uncertain situation. "What do you see as the biggest problem?"

He thought a moment. "Homelessness."

"Homelessness," Loretta mimicked Dean's radio voice. "Is that because people who aren't as fortunate as you have been screwed over by the system and can't afford basic shelter?"

"Not really," Dean said. "They just don't work hard enough. They don't want to be part of the system. So, they leech off of people who do."

After a pause, Jack said, "I see."

Loretta added, "Have I got this right? Layabout homeless people have to sleep in store doorways and muck up the neighborhood for the folks who work for a living. They probably steal change out of car consoles so they can buy food and whatever substance makes them feel better about not having a house."

"That's about it," Dean confirmed.

"Then you and Thing 1 are just the winners to figure out how to get all those criminal bums off the street."

The next instant, all five of us were standing in the middle of a forest clearing, tall trees at the perimeter and a tangle of undergrowth at our feet.

Whoa. Amid Brisa's unintelligible shouts, I couldn't help but pat down my shaking body. All the parts seemed to be there in the right places. I glanced at my friends, who were also in various stages of what-the-fuck.

I was actually relieved to hear Jack's reassuring baritone say, "To get back to where you used to be, please offer us the best solution you can as a group."

Then five backpacks—ours—hit the ground, one and two at a time. I recoiled, dancing in the leaf litter a bit until I recognized what they were.

"Okay, Hot Five!" Loretta called. "There's your stuff. Hang onto it." He pointed out the obvious. "You're officially homeless."

Chapter 9

When the shock wore off, we had to accept our fate. As the others tried to decide what to do next, I quietly had a look at the surrounding area. We couldn't be too far afield—in the here-now place, anyway—because native Douglas fir, hemlock, cedar, and sword ferns grew all around us. Semi-old growth trees, however, meant that we could be miles into whichever forest this was. Springtime birds peeped and trilled their way through evening feeding. From twenty feet up, a tiny, perturbed Douglas squirrel chattered at us, *"Pew! Pew! Pew!"*

Brisa looked up at the animal and yelled, "It's not *our* fault!" Then she eyed me. "But it is your fault, Carli. You're the one who started all this."

The gale of blame literally blew me back a step. "I—what? Jack and Loretta are the ones who called us together; not me."

She cursed in Spanish. "You answered their ridiculous question in the first place. Now they've made a habit of it."

Chris tried to smooth things over. "And these episodes follow a pattern. We solved the puzzles before. All we have to do is do that again."

Now Dean registered his displeasure. "I, for one, do not want to. As I've said, I have better things to do, especially on a Friday night."

I liked Chris's idea. "But Hamada's right, guys. If we just do as they ask, they'll let us go like before."

Dean frowned at me. "What do you care? You're grounded tonight anyway. Maybe if you would've done your civics assignment better, none of us would be having this problem."

I saw a flash of red. "Don't lecture me about grades, Mr. Flunking English."

Kavi spoke up softly, "There will be plenty of time for recriminations later. Perhaps we should focus on the job at hand. The sun, it is going down." He pointed through the boughs overhead.

Certainly, the joy of the past hour of hilarity was gone, and the day's light and warmth were fading fast. "I second the motion," I said, nodding at Kavi and putting my anger on the back burner. "Let's just get this over with."

Brisa moved toward the group of backpacks. "I don't know about you *cabrones,* but I'm gonna get my stuff." She located her robin's egg–blue bag designed like a Gucci knockoff and pulled it out of the pile. "I can't *believe* Joss made me confiscate all the cell phones—and that they are sitting in a bin backstage!"

Chris sat down cross-legged next to his pack and said, "We probably couldn't get enough bars out here to make a call anyway."

"Although they could be used to track us," Kavi informed him, "if there is even a basic signal."

"To track our dead bodies," Dean griped. "We don't even know where we are." He sat down in a huff.

"All the more reason to just answer the challenges and let Jack and Loretta airlift us out of here," Chris said. "Ideas, anyone?"

After a lull, Brisa blew out an exasperated breath. "Okay, I'll start! Let's take a bite out of crime." She gave a watery smile and tried lowering herself onto a downed tree, but jumped up again when one of the branch scars poked her behind. "I say we go with what works best and just make it worldwide. Like ... neighborhood watch!" she said definitively. "We've all seen the signs. It's, *I watch your place, you watch mine.* This keeps belongings from walking off your property. Who's with me?"

Kavi shook his head. "It is not so simple. People have to sleep." He sank to the ground and propped himself up against his humongous book bag.

"We could set up lookout times," Brisa argued.

Dean cocked his head at her. "For everyone in the world? Who's going to do that?"

She scowled. "You got a better idea?"

After a second, he snapped, "No. Does anyone? Has anybody ever solved the crime problem?"

I could kind of read between the lines. "I think that's the point, guys. The directors are asking us about the most intractable problems, hoping *we'll* find a way out of them." I leaned up against the nearest tree.

"But why us?" Chris put in.

I thought about it. "You've got to start somewhere. Maybe picking five random idiots will be like winning the lottery. Sooner or later, you find a person who thinks outside the box."

"Well," Dean countered, "we pretty much all think *inside* the box. We do what we're told to get what we want." All eyes were on him. "Like, I tried out for the play so I could pass English and get a sports scholarship."

Chris nodded. "I see what you mean. Carli answered the questions before so that we could go back to play rehearsal. Kavi here helped out the last time by identifying India's environmental problems."

Kavi responded, "These are inside of the box, yes. But as someone who must innovate to create novel electrical systems, I also think on the outer limits. I call it 'toward alternative possibilities.' In fact, I have a new, untested idea for—"

"Forget new," Brisa barked. "We need *now*. As in, a quick fix, and let's go home."

"But as I said," Kavi contested, "the trouble with crime is not so simple."

"Yes, it is!" she declared. "If you take what doesn't belong to you, you should be punished."

I faced her. "But then, how does that prevent anything? If someone has already committed a crime?"

She blinked at me. "The next time!" she roared.

Chris looked down at his lap. "So ... not a solution."

The orange glow behind the trees had deepened, and I felt a sense of urgency. Mom had always warned that a hiker shouldn't wait until dusk to either get down the mountain or make camp. "Look," I said, "we can come back to that. Let's move on. Maybe get this homeless thing in the bag first."

Nodding heads indicated the first time anyone had agreed with me all night.

***

But Dean's big issue didn't go any better. He started out by saying how money could be raised from property owners to fight the homeless. His parents, Mr. and Mrs. Dixon, were real estate agents, and the family had had this conversation at dinner every now and then.

"A parade of homeless people brings down property values in a neighborhood," he told the group. "My folks have had to handle a million transactions for families moving out of a bad area for just that reason. They lose money on their houses and have to invest more just to find a better place to live. Homeowners could actually save money by pooling donations for extra law enforcement and raids in tent camps."

Chris asked drily, "And then people won't be homeless anymore?"

Dean just looked at him. "No. Well..."

"This solves the problem only for one party," Kavi pointed out.

We went around in circles like this until we arrived at a consensus—none. There was no consensus because there were no workable solutions. This told me that trying to solve big issues by polling people one at a time was a waste of time. There had to be a better way, but I didn't know what it was.

The last rays of light flickered through the tree canopy, and I felt a pang of alarm. "People!" I started pacing. "At this rate, we'll be spending the night here."

I saw Brisa's face turn stony. *"Ay, ay, ay,"* she mumbled disconsolately.

"Looks like it," Chris said, not all that thrilled himself.

Kavi made the practical suggestion to take inventory of our supplies.

"Good idea!" Dean said, retrieving his leather backpack and unzipping the main compartment. The rest of us did the same.

Kavi said, "Okay, here is what I have," and announced the contents of his overstuffed bag: Calculus textbook and notebook; *Principles of Engineering, Volume 1*; several more textbooks; Physics syllabus and notebook; a copy of *The*

Wonderful Wizard of Oz, some loose-leaf paper and pens, a pack of peanuts, and an apple.

We all pawed through our bags and rattled off what was inside. The only thing that was common to every backpack was an apple.

"I didn't pack that," Chris mused. "Did anyone else bring an apple?"

When no one affirmed that, Brisa said, "Well, it was nice of *los jefes* to give us some dinner, no?" She took a bite out of hers.

To no one in particular, Kavi said, "I plan to save mine for later, just in case."

This impressed Brisa, who stopped chewing for a moment and replaced her piece of fruit in the front pocket of her pack. Then she voiced everybody's question: "Where the hell are we supposed to sleep?" She cast wild glances about as though searching for a nearby motel.

I let out a measured breath, trying to allay my rising anxiety. "Mom would say to find some natural shelter and carve out a wallow."

"Shit," said Chris, as the reality of our predicament set in.

"We're all gonna die," Brisa whispered.

"No, we're not," Dean stated with false confidence, his broadcasting voice nevertheless the most reassuring thing out there. He dug into his backpack for a big bottle of lukewarm Crocodile-ade and passed it around for everyone to sip. Thirst eclipsed my usual health precautions, and I took a healthy swig of the blue liquid without asking for everyone's covid status.

With what remained of the light, I searched for some high ground relative to where we were. A steep slope off to one side looked promising. "Wait here," I said to the group.

Moving off that way, I found an undercut embankment where some uprooted trees had pulled earth and stones away from the hillside. It formed a natural shelf, albeit one with eighty-foot trees growing out of the top of it. At least they appeared stable. *They had better be,* I thought. We'll be sleeping right underneath them.

I waved my arms and motioned for the other four to join me, telling them that this might be the best we could do for the night. The early-spring evening was beginning to chill, and none of us were dressed for the outdoors. I did have a thin sweater in my bag, and Dean offered to share his Pioneers jacket. Brisa clearly thought she had dibs on it, but I felt sorry for the other guys. Chris only had a short-sleeved tee, while Kavi could at least roll down the sleeves on his button-down shirt.

We each set about brushing away dirt and pebbles and sticks to clear sleeping areas. I kept hoping that Jack and Loretta would take pity on us, or appreciate our rugged resolve, or something. But as the sunlight drained away, it was clear that no one was coming to save us.

Since Dean, Brisa, Kavi, and Chris had a date to eat out after practice, and I knew I'd be going home to raid the fridge, none of us had eaten beforehand. Kavi graciously divided his peanuts up for us to share with our apples. Conversation in the semi-dark of the evening was sparse and scattered. Nobody brought up crime or homelessness again, or any topic of import. We just re-chewed the cud of our current circumstances, with some bad jokes and vague threats to quit the play after this. Finally, we gave up and decided to try and get some sleep. Brisa cozied up to Dean so they could share his coat, while the rest of us had to lie end-to-end in order to fit under the shelf.

I wriggled into my wallow and attempted to rally the troops. "It'll be okay, you guys. You'll see. Tomorrow, we'll figure all this out."

Brisa's distaste was palpable as she scooched this way and that in the damp ground, trying to get comfortable. "I hate you, Carli," she muttered, as though I were the only one who couldn't solve the crime problem or had stuck us outdoors for the night.

I tried not to think of the thousands of pounds of earth and trees above us, held up by a root system and sheer luck. I couldn't help but wonder if time was standing still, or whirling around the way it had before, so that nobody missed us. Then I wondered whether that was a good thing or a bad thing. If no one knew we were gone ... and if we couldn't find our way out of this ourselves ... who was going to help us?

***

It was hard enough sleeping when tent camping, but under the stars? I might have dozed off for a couple hours at best. Brisa's fearful narrative was not helpful. She questioned every sound, every sensation, and Dean's soothing radio voice never quieted her for long. At one point, she even gave a shriek and jumped to her feet, claiming something had slithered over her.

"Keep it in your pocket, Dixon," Chris joked lamely.

So, when gray dawn blessedly arrived, we rose, one at a time, too tired to "sleep" any longer. We rose and stomped around to warm ourselves, stretching after shivering all night.

I didn't know about Kavi, but it was probably safe to say that the rest of us had lived privileged enough lives that we had never woken up hungry or faced a day without breakfast. At least we had a little something to nibble on. Everyone but Brisa had saved half an apple; she had finished hers before turning in, so we each gave her a bite of ours, once our eyes were open and we'd worked the kinks out of our stiff bodies.

Then Brisa blurted out, "I've got to poop."

"So?" Dean replied.

She pressed her lips together and said, "No toilet paper."

After a night of hearing about bugs and dirt and possible serpents, I lost my patience. "For god's sake, Kavi, give her some notebook paper, will ya?"

We all took some, and then we weirdly all walked off in different directions looking for some privacy. We kept glimpsing each other through the trees, though, because we intuitively wanted to stick together.

Once we did our business, we drifted back to where the packs were, a little shy to have shared this human bond. I remembered the title of a kids' book I'd once seen in the library: *Everybody Poops*. It was kind of funny how we all pretended like we didn't.

An uneasy silence reigned; nobody wanted to be the first to broach the topic of our next move.

But Chris kicked open the door by saying, "I don't suppose we could just dial up Loretta and Jack and beg for mercy...."

Hope filled Brisa's squinty eyes. Dean cut Chris a nasty look.

"We could," I proposed, "but maybe we should have something to offer them in exchange."

Dean put a finger in the air. "Why not just give them the answers that me and Brisa came up with in the first place? I mean, you never know if that stuff will work until you try."

"Try *again*, you mean," Chris said.

"Yeah, if either of those old, worn-out ideas worked, we wouldn't be having this conversation," I remarked. "Besides, they asked for a group decision. As in, something we agree on." I paused, then added bluntly, "And running ICE raids on homeless people and turning neighbors into informants are stupid ideas."

"Well, we agree on that," Chris murmured, earning glares from Dean and B.

Kavi hadn't said a word since we'd finished our apples. He raised a hand to get our attention. "You know, I have been working on an experimental method of objectively reaching the most viable plan of action for any given—"

"Oh, shut *up*, Kavi!" Brisa snapped at him. "Nobody cares about your dumb systems analysis for something as simple as just plain communicating. We all know how to do it. You people are just stubborn."

"Well, I..." He seemed to recede into the ground beneath his feet.

This made me mad. "Hey. He was just trying to help."

Dean started zipping compartments on his backpack and said, "Well, you folks can debate all you want. I'm getting out of here."

Even though this pronouncement held no promise of success, just hearing it made us feel better. It would be preferable to do something rather than nothing. Wordlessly, the rest of us gathered our things.

We all hesitated, waiting for someone else to take the lead. There were no clear, definitive directions that might take us out of the forest and back to civilization. There wasn't even a damn deer path that I could make out in the yellowing dawn. Then I remembered something else Mom had said about wilderness hiking.

I put up both hands. "Shh! Quiet a sec." I thought I heard what I was listening for. But was it a trickle of water, or just the morning breeze through the fir needles? Well, it was a possibility anyway.

I turned on my heel and gestured. "This way. Follow me."

Chapter 10

We did come across a creek in a few minutes of walking, the welcome sound of it growing louder the closer we came. "There it is, ladies and gentlemen," I announced.

Brisa said, "Good, 'cause I'm thirsty!" She began to climb the tangle of roots and underbrush to get to the water.

Chris called out, "But you might not want to drink that, B."

She kept going and tossed over her shoulder, "Why not?"

"Giardia," I supplied.

She slowed her steps. "What the heck is that?"

"Ah!" Kavi put up a hand. "This I can tell you. It is a microscopic parasite that invades the intestines and causes sickness and even death."

Now Brisa stopped. "Wait. What?" She looked back at the running creek. "But it's so fresh and clean. Pure mountain water and all that." Still, she hesitated.

"Those beautiful mountain streams are tainted by beaver poop," I told her. "When Mom goes backpacking, she takes these special tablets to purify water, since she can't exactly carry a case of Asano."

"And she wouldn't be able to recycle all those empty plastic bottles," Chris added wryly.

"In the small towns of India," Kavi went on, "many wells are contaminated, and of course the big waterways also are."

"I thought those rivers were sacred," Dean said, recalling something Kavi had mentioned when we flew over the Ganges the previous week. "Does that mean when people are bathing and washing clothes in there that they're in some kind of parasitic soup?"

Kavi's voice got hushed. "It is an accepted practice for people to go to the bathroom in running water as well." More matter-of-factly, he said, "Our environmental challenges come from all sides."

"For god's sake, man," Dean put in. "Why don't you get 'em to stop?"

Kavi drew himself up to his full, modest height. "As you well know, it takes time to change people's behavior."

"But it can be done," Chris said optimistically. "Look at, say, smoking. Or picking up dog poop. People used to do whatever they wanted, even though it bothered lots of other folks. Now there are no-smoking laws and leash and poop laws. You're considered a jerk if you don't follow them, but for sure, that took decades to get people on board."

Brisa had returned to the rest of us. "Then why, may I ask, did you want to find this stream, Carlita?"

"Mom says if you get lost in the mountains, find a stream and follow it downhill." All this talk of water was making me thirsty. "But in our case, if it dumps into a larger river, there might be marked trails there that will take us to a road out of here. Or maybe we can find some hikers who will help us."

"So, what do we do for water in the meantime?" Dean asked. We had emptied his Crocodile-ade bottle first thing this morning.

Kavi's eyebrows hunched lower over his dark eyes. "Good question."

After a moment, we all started to move downstream, picking our way over the flora. Here, near the water, grew red alder and Western hemlock trees, and some kind of willow. Reedy horsetail and lush ferns clogged the banks, and the odd rhododendron shrub surprised us with pinkish blooms. A kingfisher cried somewhere upstream, and a couple of indigo Steller's jays scolded us as we walked along.

We kept it up as long as we could, but finally our way was blocked by massive downed trees that stretched across the waterway.

"Now what?" Brisa called to me, as though daring me not to have an answer.

I gauged the extent of the obstacle. "We're not getting around that."

Kavi suggested, "Perhaps it will be easier going on the other side of the creek."

I looked to where he pointed, but whether that was any clearer was anybody's guess. "We could cross to that side...."

"Or," said Dean, "we could backtrack upslope and try to rejoin the water further downstream. It'd be like portaging, only without canoes."

Our sporty friend did have some experience in the outdoors. In the course of our conversations, Dean had described family and club camping trips, and of course, he had been skiing locally and in the Alps—probably Aspen and Tahoe as well.

From the look on Brisa's face, she did not relish crossing the stream over the largest downed cedar tree, even though it was at least two feet wide. Branches still stuck up from it, and a misstep could cause a tangle and a fall. "I vote for going around," she said firmly.

The rest of us didn't want a fight, and both options had about even chances of success ... or failure. So, we turned around and headed back, fading in the downstream direction little by little as we pushed through the bushes.

At one point, I cut a look at the rest of the crew. Brisa was trying hard to keep it together, the forward motion giving her something to focus on. Chris soldiered on, deep in thought, while Kavi, heavily laden with his backpack, struggled over vines that begged tripping. Dean, in his Pioneers letter jacket, had a sheen of sweat on his face and neck, but his long legs made good time and easily forked over any fallen logs in their way. Then I caught some reflected light near the ground ahead.

"Come on, guys! There it is." I pointed at the tributary we had rejoined.

Kavi eyed the banks, which were steep and littered with tangled forest debris. There was no beach access. It looked to be tougher going than we had just left behind. "You know," he said, "we do not have to travel directly alongside this stream. Perhaps a bit further from the water will be less congested."

We all surveyed both directions, and he was right. So, I led us downstream, close enough to hear the water but far enough to avoid the pile-ups.

After a while, we all needed a break.

"Does anyone know what time it is?" Brisa asked. "I miss my phone!"

Only Kavi among us was wearing a wristwatch. "It is 8:47."

Ugh. Was that all? It seemed like we'd been traveling all day. Getting up before the crack of dawn would do that to you. "Let's take a time out," I proposed. "I'm exhausted already."

This perked Brisa up. Our assistant director mimicked Malia Kendrake playing Kate Hardcastle, reciting, "I second the motion! As Shakespeare or Dexter or somebody once said, 'Would it were bedtime, and all were well.'"

***

Around eleven-ish, it began to drizzle. At the first drops, Brisa yelped. Kavi began periodically wiping his eyeglasses off with his shirt. My heart sank. I wanted to put on my sweater but realized if it got wet, it would only be harder to dry off.

"I hate to say this, folks, but we're going to have to take cover."

"No way!" Dean countered. "If we keep on, we'll have a breakthrough. We *are* heading in the right direction, right?"

Who could tell? But if I wanted them to follow me—and they needed to follow someone—I'd have to project confidence. "Of course! Downstream. Downhill. To a main tributary and a main road." That was as far as I could take the act, though. "Seriously, we don't want to get soaked to the skin. Not good."

"You can borrow my coat," Dean said, trying to persuade me.

"We can't all wear your coat, and the guys don't have anything else to put on." I shrugged at Kavi and Chris, who appeared uncomfortable but weren't complaining. Yet.

So, again, we searched for some shelter and found a good dry spot beneath some closely grouped hemlock trees. Their feathery branches spread over us like a loose roof.

With our own efforts on hold, Kavi advocated another round of Let's Make a Consensus Deal, and nobody could refuse. At least we agreed on that. And it would take our minds off of our growling stomachs and dry mouths. This time, he took the lead.

"Rather than posing solutions to crime and the homeless situation," he began, "suppose we first ask why these problems exist? A better understanding of this may generate some more in-depth responses toward alternative possibilities."

Why did he have to be right so often?

This discussion took up the better part of an hour. We seesawed between casting blame on the perpetrators and the government, and talking about what a perfect world would look like without these problems. This still did not get us to a unanimous agreement on either issue.

We could hear heavier raindrops hitting the soft, green hemlock needles and the ground outside the circle of trees. It looked like we were either going to have to stay put indefinitely or hike out, weather be damned. The antsy Dean convinced us to move on, suggesting we trade off wearing his coat. That was enough incentive, and we drew conifer needles to see who would get to warm up first.

Kavi won that round. The relief in his eyes, even behind the rain-dotted glasses, was evident. Still, the rest of us would have to go unprotected—I'd decided to save my dry sweater for later. Mom had instilled in me a healthy respect for hypothermia, a real possibility, even on a day with temperatures in the fifties. The thermometer would plunge after dark, and who knew where we'd be then? We took turns going off to pee under another set of trees before we left.

While Brisa was off in the bushes, Chris noticed a shiny, yellow wrapper sticking out of a corner of her backpack's front pouch. "What's that?" he called our attention to it; the color was striking in the dim light beneath our shelter.

Dean didn't mind reaching into her pack for it. "Whoa-ho-ho-ho!" He held up an open, party-sized bag of candy. "Peanut M&Ms, on me!"

We were all pretty hungry by now, and who doesn't like Peanut M&Ms? He passed them around, and everybody took a handful. We were happily munching when Brisa returned.

Her eyes narrowed as she spotted the half-empty bag on Chris's lap.

"Hamada! Give it." She thrust out a hand. "And give the rest back. They're mine." She reached over to where Dean was crouched and tried to swipe the chocolate and peanut nuggets out of his palm, but most ended up on the ground.

Brisa lunged for him. Dean jerked his hand back. Meanwhile, Kavi knelt down and began picking up the errant candies.

Chris and I just watched in semi-horror. First of all, we had never seen a physical altercation over Peanut M&Ms. Second, Dean Dixon had had the temerity to take them out of Brisa's bag and hand them out. And third, it dawned on all of us that Brisa had not included said candy in the collective inventory of our backpacks.

Kavi stood up and called for the two to stop their little slap-fight. He looked angry for the first time I'd seen. "It is clear you have concealed from us, Brisa, this important food source and have been hoarding it for yourself." He took one of her hands and turned it palm-up. "Here!" He gave her the dozen or so M&Ms he'd retrieved from the dirt. "Since you are so obsessed with your *property*." Then he stalked off to use the latrine.

It was my turn to feel hurt. "B.," I said, holding back tears. We might not have been starving yet, but no one knew where our next meal was coming from. "How could you? We're your friends."

She had brushed off the candies and popped them in her mouth. Now the taste must have soured, for her jaws clenched and she looked as though she might spit them out. "They're mine," she repeated in a small voice through the chewed-up peanuts and chocolate.

"Another example of rampant property theft," Chris retorted acidly.

"Yeah. I know how we could've solved that," I said. "You *share*."

***

As if by magic, the rain stopped just then. Had I said something right?

To hedge our bets, we turned to the topic of homelessness as we again blazed a trail in tandem with the stream. The four of us treated Brisa coldly but politely, letting her comment but not addressing her directly.

Dean again regaled us with the ramifications of ubiquitous street people on homeowners, and Chris talked about the inhumane and often unsanitary conditions of urban tent camps.

Once more, Kavi let his frustration surface. "But what of the underlying concepts? I thought we had agreed to identify those."

So, I brought up America's taboo on dealing with mental health, as so many homeless individuals wound up on the street because they went untreated and couldn't deal with everyday tasks, let alone get jobs.

Dean tried to argue with me. "Thriftwell hires people like that."

"Which won't make a dent in the number of mentally disabled," Chris said. "Besides, a lot of them have addictions, and nobody will hire them."

"My cousin Shelly got hooked on some kind of generic oxy," Brisa announced. "She had shoulder surgery and got a prescription. She goes in and out of rehab, and that's, like, her life now."

"She is lucky to have this rehab," Kavi reasoned. "It is a home, no?"

"Look," I said. "Some people are just plain poor. Or their rent went up. Or they lost a job and had a lot of credit card bills. I saw this movie where all of those things happened. The lady went from having property, to living in a hotel, to living in her car. When she finally had to sell her car to eat, it was sleeping in doorways for her."

"Sad," Dean agreed.

Just then, I noticed that the sound of running water had gotten louder. And after twenty-five more yards, louder still. My heart started beating faster. I broke away and crashed through the trees, heading for the stream we'd been paralleling. "Hey!" I yelled. "There's a fork in the stream!"

The fork angled off into a bigger, wider creek—not quite a river, but not really a creek anymore. I got no arguments about turning off to follow it.

We did this for a long time, zigzagging around boulders, decaying logs, and stands of alder trees, with their insect-riddled oval leaves shedding rainwater. We had moved from dense conifer forest to a partial riparian area, and now to an even more open environment. It looked familiar ... and the farther we went, the wider and faster the body of water flowed. At this point, I could call it a river. What I wasn't ready for, though, was what I saw next: a T-post–and–wire fence that bounded a wide, green lawn, with a structure at the far side of it.

A house.

Chapter 11

"¡Jesus, María, y José!" exclaimed Brisa, falling to her knees as though she were starring in a telenovela. The rapid Spanish that followed needed no translation, as its tone perfectly articulated our collective reaction to re-entry into civilization.

Kavi also displayed more drama than usual. "We are saved!" he said quietly, the anticipation in his eyes speaking much more loudly. He shrugged out of Dean's coat and returned it to him.

Chris reached over and wordlessly squeezed my hand. Dean put on his jacket, rearranged his pack over his shoulder, and made for the fence line.

I don't know what was holding me back from the elation shown by the others. True, I had always been the cautious sort; Dad used to joke that if money fell from the sky, I would open a savings account before grabbing any of it. Maybe it came from being an only child without any siblings to protect me. And maybe the pandemic had heightened my natural carefulness. But, as Brisa got up and hurried after Dean, I called, *"Espérate, chica!* Hold up, Dixon." They glanced back at me. "Let's think this through."

Dean waved me away. "What's to think?" He approached the fence and appeared to be searching for a way over the wire squares, which wouldn't hold his weight, when a large dog came barreling across the wide lawn that spread between the fence and the house. It barked continuously in a sort of sonar radar that bounced off of each of us, enumerating the potential trespassers before we could breach the perimeter.

The dog looked to be some sort of German shepherd cross, and its hackles were up. Dean stopped short on the safe side of the four-foot-high fence, and we all hoped it was tall enough to contain the beast. I glanced back the way it had come, to the back side of a modest, brown-painted house with wooden siding and darker brown trim around the windows, their panes reflecting the late-afternoon sun. A single story reached out toward a matching, detached garage and a few mismatched outbuildings. On the other side of those, several vehicles were parked—two pickups, an older sedan, and a motor home, the kind with a spare compartment in the back for a runaround vehicle.

Then I saw what I was looking for: a coil of green garden hose hanging near the back door. I nudged Chris's elbow and pointed at it.

"Yes!" He started eyeing the fence line to see how to get over there. "Come on! Let's try going around." He motioned us to follow him, and we let the dog go bonkers on its side of the fence as we paralleled the house.

It was messy going. The unfenced area that led down to the river was wet from spring rains, and weeds pressed against the T-posts where someone hadn't yet used the electric trimmer this season. The barking didn't let up. We found a corner and turned toward the house. Now I could see more vehicles clustered around a gravel driveway—two newer sedans, an old van, and a couple of cargo trailers. That was a lot of tires, I thought, and then, next to the house, I spied a barbecue grill on wheels and a collection of wheeled trash cans. There ought to be some sort of conveyance that could carry us out of here.

Poor Kavi was hustling to keep up with the rest of us, shifting his big bookbag around on his back and pushing his glasses up on his sweaty nose. He kept a nervous eye on the apoplectic dog, and then gave a yelp himself as his foot hit a hole and he went down on one knee. I hung back and waited for him to catch up.

We skirted the side yard and drew near the next fence corner, where a large gate gave access to the back for a tractor or lawn mower. I was wondering how we could get to the hose with that dog loose in there when an angry voice called from the depths of the open garage, "That's far enough!"

We nearly all bumped into each other, we halted so fast. The sky was overcast, and the garage interior dark. There was no telling who that voice belonged to.

Dean, with his long legs, had taken the lead, and now purported to speak for our group. "It's just us," he said in his baritone, as though everyone should know who we were. "Can you get hold of your dog?"

"We'd like to use your hose, please," I added, the reedy tenor of desperation in my voice.

"You fucking people," the voice returned. "Get out!"

This was not what we'd expected to hear. Then came the unmistakable *chock-chock* of a rifle being cocked.

***

Back in the day, Mom had told Dad and I tales of landowners threatening and running off hikers near the national scenic trail. People would wander off the footpath to try to get a phone signal or find a road to a town where they could replenish their supplies. Not all of the locals were cool with that, and during heavy-use times, they might be justified in their impatience with the number of interlopers. But we weren't your ordinary hikers. We were five high-school and college kids who were hungry, thirsty, and lost.

As we all froze in our tracks, Dean tried to convey this information to get some leniency from our foe.

His authoritative broadcaster's voice, with a hint of fearful urgency, seemed appropriate. "We're just from Foster High. We could use some—"

The ominous voice again cut him off. "You freeloaders! Get away from my vehicles. Get off my land!" Hearing its master's alarm, the dog in the backyard alternated between barking and sinister growls.

Dean tried to correct the first impression. "You don't understand—we're not freeloaders. We're on a mission and we need a ride—"

Kavi tugged at Dean's arm. "Stop! I think he thinks you're... Get back here and let someone else do the talking!" He jutted his chin at Chris.

It dawned on Dean that our friend Hamada had the preferred coloring, and he quickly dropped back to hover with Kavi, Brisa, and me behind Chris.

The surly voice from the garage did sound like a White man's. "This is private property. Now, get moving."

I couldn't have moved if I'd wanted to. That feeling of tiny needles poking my entire body had returned, this time from fear. I knew I should speak up, but Chris beat me to it.

"S-sir..." he croaked. "We're not after your things. We've gotten lost. We need some help."

Inanely, I piped up, "Our folks'll vouch for us if you just let us use your phone."

"You look like common thugs," came the reply. "Got your backpacks for whatever you can carry."

Dean tried again from the background. "My jeep is parked back at school. I'm graduating next month. I've got a scholarship...."

The tone of voice didn't change. "Of course you do," the man spat from inside the garage. "Special treatment. People like you are why people like my boy can't *get* scholarships."

Kavi grabbed Dean by his pack, and I soundlessly mouthed, *No!*

I took a step forward. "If you'll just give us some water and tell us where we are, we'll go," I promised.

"I owe you nothing! Now, get out before I call the sheriff."

"Please!" Brisa pleaded. "Can't we just use your hose?"

He answered this request with a rifle shot—we could see a flash in the dark garage, and the blast was deafening.

We all dropped to the ground, but the bullet must have shied off into the woods. I reached for my best friend, grabbed her hand, and pulled her after me. "Come on! Go, go, go!"

We had no choice but to run out into the trees, hoping our retreat would be enough to save us from the man's wrath.

Ohmygod, ohmygod, ohmygod... Every cell of my body had ignited, adrenaline pushing me past a place where I might get shot toward any other place on Earth. Dean streaked by. I lost ahold of Brisa's hand, and she and Chris stumbled along just behind me.

"Wait!"

It was Kavi. He thundered up to us, having ditched his backpack, his shirt untucked and flapping behind him.

"I have dropped my things!" he panted.

"Let's just keep going for now," Chris puffed at him.

We ran through the trees, stumbling over vines and ferns, dodging low-hanging limbs, and leaping clumps of rocks and sticks. Suddenly, Brisa fell heavily, with a shriek.

"Are you okay?" I yelled, slowing, but she had already rocked to her feet and moved unsteadily after me.

"I'm good," she said, and we all slowed and stopped to encircle her.

I bent at the waist, hands on my knees, trying to get some wind. Kavi sank to the ground. His glasses were missing, and he breathed in heavy spurts.

"Holy shit." Dean, in his heavy athletic jacket, streamed sweat as he threw down his pack.

"Ay, Carli," Brisa said, swiping an arm around my shoulders and beginning to cry. We held each other there for a minute, the futility of tears and sweat finally separating us.

Chris was consoling Kavi, and Dean stared off into space with a look on his face that I'd never seen before. Under his breath, he whispered, "I have a scholarship...." as though it would somehow protect him.

Each of us fell quiet, until the sound of our breathing and distant barking was all we could hear. We'd lost track of the river. We had crossed no road. We were more lost than ever, if that were even possible.

***

Although becoming a bull's-eye was a first for me, what filled my mind as we rested was that I had never before been targeted for the way I looked. It's true that many Cuban Americans get to choose whether they are white or Hispanic on any given day. My biggest tell was a small beauty mark just above my lip, a feature common to Cuban islanders of Spanish heritage. On a skin-color scale of light to dark, the Hot Five sequence was pale Chris, me, Brisa, Kavi, and then Dean, who was still within the milk chocolate, not the molasses, range. Chris, with his paper-white complexion, won the spokesman prize with an angry white man, despite the Asian Hamada genes. Nonthreatening, you know.

Of everything that had just transpired—from an attack dog to an armed confrontation and a mad dash through an unfamiliar forest—being struck with the factor of race was what scared me the most. Who was I really?

"Can you believe that dickhead?" Dean finally said. "What do we look like, some kind of gang?"

"More like an ad for health insurance," Chris said sarcastically, meaning our multicultural breakdown for optimal product placement.

Kavi seemed overwhelmed. "In London, this does not happen," he said, as though he still didn't believe it. "Yes, there might be a slur against one's country of origin, but not..."

"Having a brown face?" Brisa finished for him, disgusted. "*Yo sé, pero* in America, it's a big thing."

"But look what's behind it," I said. "The guy thought we were there to steal his stuff—carjackers or barbecue grill hijackers, or whatever." I paused. "I guess that's what people like him expect from— " I narrowed my eyes. "—people like us."

Chris said in a low voice, "I'm sorry, guys. In lots of other settings, I'm ... people like you." I could see him mentally reliving the grade-school taunts he had surely received for being "Chinese," even though his mom was White.

I can't explain it, but somehow this shared bigotry unified us in a way that not even being part of a stage play could.

"This is distasteful," Kavi said, "but being shot at is a first in my book. The ratio of guns to people in America is the main reason why my mother did not want me to come here, even though she at the same time wants me to get an American education." He sighed. "In London, I am not running away from insane gunmen."

"What about you, Dixon?" Chris broached the subject with Dean. "Did your parents ever have 'the talk' with you? I hear that's a rite of passage."

Dean nodded. "The 'what to do if you're pulled over by White cops' talk is a popular one. But we only heard it in passing, my brother, Farrell, and me. We've always been in right places at the right time."

"What does this mean?" Kavi asked.

Brisa said, "People of color are more likely to be wiped out by cops for no good reason. So, parents tell their kids—usually the guys, but girls too—how to act, not to be confrontational, not to run away. That kind of thing."

Without his glasses, I could easily see the recognition in Kavi's eyes. "This I understand. But what are the right places and time?"

Dean answered, "Our family is lucky. We can orchestrate those things. Like, my parents started the first all–African American realty company on our side of town. We see Black people, they're comfortable with us, we're comfortable with them. But we also travel to the kind of 'White' places where we are accepted—what some might say is where the jet-set goes."

"You mean," I put in, "if you see Black people acting like they belong in Aspen or some fancy hotel, they figure you're the 'good' kind? The Hollywood kind?"

He eyed me. "Something like that."

In a way, this was all so visceral and in-your-face. But in a way, it was theoretical and pedestrian—at least, by comparison with our immediate situation. Who gave a crap what the census would say about us? We were still lost in the damn woods.

"I'm soooo thirsty," Brisa moaned.

We all were. "We've got to get back to the river," I insisted.

"What about the giardia?" Dean reminded me.

"Who cares? Priorities, man. We need water, and it's getting late."

"Jesus, what if we're out here another night?" Chris lamented.

"We don't even know where the road is from here," Brisa said. "And if I don't get a drink pretty soon, I'm gonna collapse."

"Okay," I said. "Show of hands. I say we go back to the river first, then either find the road or find some shelter. Agreed?"

Their hands went up.

"And after that," I continued, "we can and will satisfy Jack and Loretta's demand." I glanced at Kavi. "You and I will double back and pick up your pack and try to find your glasses." I turned to the rest of them. "All of us will be thinking about the underlying reasons for crime and homelessness. Then we can come up with some solutions." I paused. "One way or another, we *will* get out of here in one piece."

Brisa smiled at me, the way she used to smile at me. "Okay. Except for one thing. We're gonna need some energy." She reached for her backpack and unzipped the front compartment. "Peanut M&Ms, anyone?"

Chapter 12

And just like that—*poof!*—Jack and Loretta invaded our heads again, lifting us out of the woods and making their point about crime and homelessness. It was going to take wide-scale agreement and a sense of generosity to get any meaningful changes. The directors even threw in Kavi's backpack and glasses when they returned us to the FCC stage. But they did not immediately release us into the wilds of the theater. The stage remained dark, and we remained immobilized.

The Hot Five were certainly relieved to be safe again, but no one expressed gratitude at that. In fact, Brisa was pissed.

"That's it! I've had enough!" she yelled at our unseen captors. "None of these things are my *problemas* to solve."

"Ah, ah, ah," Jack warned duskily. "It's talk like that that got you on our list in the first place."

"List?" I screeched. "You've got a list? And a bunch of amateur thespians are at the top of it?"

Loretta clucked at our ignorance. "It's a metaphor, guys. No one thinks it's up to them to tackle world crises. And until everybody does, they'll just fester, like Brisa's slow-burning defensiveness."

I could almost feel B.'s ears get hot. "Leave her alone!" I said. "We all have our personal ... stuff."

Loretta picked right up on that. "And that's the problem, isn't it? Stuff." He puffed into the microphone a bit. "Tell you what. You've had a long couple of days. Jack and I are going to let you ruminate about the nature and complications of your possessions and how fixating on them affects others." Under his breath, he muttered, "Jesus, you humans are so shallow...." before clicking off and leaving us in the dark.

Kavi's even tone rose in the blackness. "I believe the implication is that economic distribution is both the root of those two problems and the cure."

After a beat, Dean said, "You mean, like, possessions are important to rich people because they can always get more, and they're important to poor people because they are always dangling just out of reach? So, a better balance could shift things?"

Chris mimicked a game show host: "Ding! Ding! Ding! Tell the man what he's won, Johnny." To Dean, he said, "Consider this the moral of the M&Ms story."

It was odd how Jack and Loretta's concepts came to life in ways that even Dean Dixon could understand. But how were we to tell the world? Basically, everyone had to get on board for people to make any progress. And we knew that was an impossible dream.

I asked my friends how we could ever break that barrier in our lifetimes, or even the lifetimes of generations to come.

"Never happen," Dean concluded fatalistically.

"You know," Chris mused, "a better way to reach everyone on Earth would help."

"Yeah," Brisa replied, "it's called the Internet, *niño.*"

"*Better* than the Internet," Chris insisted.

We were quiet a second while everyone pondered what that might be. Then Kavi spoke up again.

"One obstacle is the sheer number of people who must be connected. But more compelling is the need for them to communicate honestly with each other. Then there is the complicating factor of asking them to address issues based on facts rather than wishes or emotions."

"What? That's how I always solve my problems," Brisa said. "I go with my gut."

"You do know," Chris put in, "that guts weren't designed for analytical thinking, right?"

Kavi cleared his throat in the darkness. "This is why I have developed an objective means of—"

"Whatever!" Brisa exclaimed. "Duke it out with yourselves. I'm done with this crap. I don't have to be here, and I'm getting off the crew list. Joss can find another AD."

I was stunned; Brisa rarely backed down on anything, let alone a bossy role like assistant director in a very cool play. "No way, B.!"

Now Dean sounded upset. "You can't just quit, Breese. Rehearsals wouldn't be the same without you."

A frantic note entered her voice. "You're just saying that because you need the extra credit for doing the play. Because *you* want something. Well, I want to get on with my life, without having to risk it every time the stage goes dark."

Just then, we heard laughter, and as the footlights came up, our fellow cast and crew members became visible. Somebody sailed a prop tray across the stage like a Frisbee, and then Joss stomped over to the wings and activated the air horn to get the cast's attention, but I could see she was smiling too. I vaguely recalled we'd been fooling around in the middle of Act Two.

To regroup, Joss called for a break, but asked everyone to stay in their places for a moment—which was easy for me to do, considering every voluntary muscle fiber of mine had basically melted upon returning from our little ... field trip. I was lucky I still had control of my involuntary ones.

I surreptitiously surveyed my body, which seemed intact, and then glanced over at the rest of the Hot

Five. We were back to our usual appearances, minus the effects of forty-eight hours outdoors running around in the wilderness. Our backpacks lay where we'd stowed them, at the foot of the stage-left wing curtains, our phones in their offstage bin—I could hear somebody's burbling faintly over there.

Joss reached into that area and brought out a couple items, then faced the cast and crew. There were Mason and Dave B., fresh off their scene with Blaze as Constance. Malia and the servant girls sat on folding chairs at the back of the stage, with the rest of the cast and crew members out in the audience seats.

"*¡Jefe!*" Joss mustered Brisa. "Come here." She addressed the rest of us. "Us angels are halfway through six weeks of hell, and I want to recognize my assistant director, without whom I would be stuck in purgatory." She handed Brisa a little gift bag as she placed something on her head. It was a silver birthday tiara from the Two-Bucks store. "Ladies and gentlemen, your assistant director, Brisa Morales!"

Being in a rare mood, they gave her a thunderous round of applause.

I slid my eyes at hers and pressed my lips into a grin. *Just try to quit now, amiga.*

***

Of all times, my first big scene with Chris and Dave B. was coming up, when what I wanted was to be home in bed. Yet, I didn't feel tired or stressed as though I had just run for my life through the woods. Every time this *thing* happened and the directors returned us to the stage, I wondered if I had imagined it all. But then I realized that I brought back things I hadn't had beforehand—a plastic bottle, say, or this time, insights. I'd have to channel some of that into my performance.

But first, Spider Marlow had to meet his blind date.

"Places!" Brisa bellowed from beneath her crown, and Malia's Kate faced Mason's Spider, ready to completely misunderstand each other. His wingman, Hastings, introduced the two.

Dave B. swept an arm at the couple and said disingenuously, "I'm proud of bringing two persons of such merit together, who have no ulterior motives whatsoever." He blinked at the audience for a laugh.

As they enter, Miss Kate Hardcastle tries to tamp down her wild demeanor, while Spider Marlow looks like he's tied up in knots on the inside and might vomit at any minute. Malia did this by putting a hat over her multihued hair, and Mason projected a very constipated expression. But Malia did her streetwalker impression again, definitely giving off mixed signals.

Miss Hardcastle said to herself, "Now to meet my modest gentleman with a *sedate* face, so as not to freak him out." Then she approached Spider. "Hey, sweet and sexy—I mean, kind sir. You made it. My brother says you took a detour on the way."

Spider decided that Kate looked wenchlike enough. "A detour? Only to the pub, madam." Mason eyed her up and down. "You know, your natural habitat."

Dave B. leaned over to him and continued the wingman act. "You never spoke better in your whole life, dude. Keep razzing her," he encouraged. "Women love that."

Miss Hardcastle: "You flatter me, sir. To think that someone like you, who probably drinks beer out of a fancy bottle, could lower yourself to my level."

Marlow, salaciously: "Oh, I can go even lower."

Miss Hardcastle, demure: "A hard partier, like you, Mr. Spider, would have much to teach me, I am sure."

Marlow eyed her again: "Oh, I doubt that. You look like you've been rode hard and put away wet more than a few times."

This got a good laugh from the onlookers. The back-and-forth continued, with Spider thinking Kate is a woman of ill repute, and her believing she's disguised herself well enough to be taken for an ingenue. They agree to meet later to exchange bodily fluids, leaving Kate certain that she can bend the would-be lawyer to her will and make her parking tickets disappear forever.

That was my cue. I didn't wait for Brisa to announce an entrance but followed Chris and Blaze as they moved to center stage. Dave B. glided after me.

"Places! Props!" The prop master handed me a clean protective facemask.

More subterfuge and misinterpretations were coming our way. My "son"—Chris as Tony—was

edging away from the advances of my "niece"—
Blaze's Constance—all for show. The two trooped
forward in single file, and Chris pretended that Tony
was appalled. "What are you following me around
so closely for, Cousin Con? You should be ashamed
of yourself."

Blaze rubbed right up against him. "Can't a girl
cozy up to her own relations these days?"

Chris jumped back. "I know what sort of relations
you're looking for, but you're barking up the wrong
tree. For one thing, I'm still social-distancing. Give
me some space!"

The two of them faded toward the drawing room
backdrop—or where it would be, once the set crew
finished painting it. Kavi brought up a spotlight on
Dave B. and me, and I fell hard into Mrs. Hardcastle's
mindset. She was clearly flirting with the younger
man.

"Well! I vow, Mr. Hastings, you are very
entertaining," I said shrilly, being more off-putting
than seductive. "I love nothing in the world so much
as talk of New York and the fashions, though I was
never there myself."

Hastings, too, was putting up a façade, meant to both impress and dis the old lady. "Never been to New York! You amaze me! From your airs and manner, I concluded you had spent your entire life at the Waldorf Astoria."

Of course, she didn't get it. "O! sir," I said with false modesty, "we are but country persons. I do take care to know all the fashions as they come out, however." I preened in my mask. "Pray, how do you like this elegant N95, Mr. Hastings?"

This got a chuckle from offstage.

Dave B. said, "Extremely elegant and degagée, upon my word, madam," and I couldn't help but cut a look over at Brisa upon hearing the French word.

This earned a note from Joss. "Focus, Mrs. Hardcastle!"

Hastings continued to dis her. "Such an ... *improvement* to your looks must surely draw as many gazers as Lady Gaga!"

I just batted my eyes.

Dave B. leaned closer. "But I must compliment you on your necklace, Mrs. Hardcastle. I've never seen anything like it."

I faked showing it to him. "It is a golden wrench—a family heirloom. Studded with rubies and emeralds. It's to be my niece's when she turns twenty-one." This brought Tony and Constance back into the picture. As they approached, I explained to Hastings, "They fall in and out of love ten times a day, as if they were man and wife already." To Chris, I said, "Well, Tony, child, what soft things are you saying to your cousin Constance this evening?"

Tony complained, "Nothing soft; it's very hard to be followed about all the time. I can't get a moment to myself anywhere in this house but the john."

Blaze's Miss Neville kept up the ruse of pursuing him: "Then I'll know where to look for you next time you're hiding from your mother. I do know my way around the plumbing, you know," she added suggestively.

Easily fooled, I said, "Ah! he's a sly one. Always thinking of your family business. Wouldn't he make a fine ... *partner*, Constance?" I reached for Blaze's hand. "Take a look, Mr. Hastings, what a handsome couple they make." I held out my other hand to Chris and snatched at his. "Come, Tony."

He jerked away. "You can't make me!" They went on to argue about his small inheritance.

I feigned tears in my eyes. "Ungrateful boy! You deserve neither that nor the golden wrench that will unlock the Neville riches."

Spider's wingman came to the rescue. "Dear madam," Hastings intervened, "permit me to lecture the young gentleman a little. I'm certain I can persuade him of his duty."

This, my Mrs. Hardcastle accepted. "Well, I leave him in your capable hands, sir. Come, Constance, my love. I have some more fascinating lint sculptures to show you." And we exited, stage-right.

***

Nailed it! Boy, was I jazzed up. Dave B. mouthed, *Awesome!*

Brisa strode over, took my hand, and pulled me to a chair near the wing to watch the rest of the scene. "That was so great, Carli," she murmured with admiration. I could see she was back in her element, back to loving this so much she couldn't quit. Besides, she was wearing a tiara. Royalty didn't *get* to quit.

The end of the scene was a set-up for the whole rest of the play. Lazy Tony Lumpkin needs a way out of an arranged marriage, and Beau Hastings needs a way to extricate his boo, Constance, from the clutches of Tony's family. So, they make a deal.

Tony said to Beau, "Don't mind my mother, man. Let her cry. I've seen her and sister Kate cry over a chick flick for two hours. When I asked them what was wrong, they said the more the movie made them cry, the better they liked it. So I bring them to tears every chance I get."

Dave B. drew back and sized Chris up. "I'm guessing you're no friend to the ladies, then, Tony. Am I right?"

"That's safe to say." Chris wiggled his eyebrows in emphasis.

"And your mother is completely unaware of this?"

"I've given her every hint." Chris skipped across the stage and back. "She won't take them. Keeps trying to throw Cousin Con and me together."

Dave B. put hands on hips. "Well, there must be someone you've got your eye on...."

"Sure," Tony said. "You've met, down at the pub."

Beau paused, then guessed, "That bartender at the Naked Parrot?" Tony nodded and Beau Hastings continued, "What say you to a friend that would take this bitter bargain off your hands?"

Tony eyed him. "You mean Connie? Take, man! Take!"

Hastings thought it over. "I'll tell you what. If you help me out, I'll smuggle your cousin off to the next state, and you'll never hear from her again."

Chris played a man who couldn't believe his good fortune. Beside himself, Tony said, "Help you out! You bet, to the last drop of my blood. I'll go out and charge your Tesla, grab Ma's necklace, and you and Connie can ride off into the sunset, or just past sunset. Cover of darkness and all, you know. May the golden wrench and all of the rights and privileges associated with it be yours!"

Thus ended Act Two.

Brisa and I received a buoyed Chris with hugs as he exited, and he and I gravitated to Dean and Kavi while Brisa went to return everyone's cellphones.

"Good stuff, people!" Joss called. "It's really shaping up. See you next week."

It must have been nice to be so sure of that.

"*Will* we see you next week?" Dean asked Brisa as she finished her task and met us at the backpack pile.

She picked up the gift bag Joss had given her and tipped her tiara at a jaunty angle. "Looks like I'll be here," she said with a smile.

"Well, how about tomorrow night then?" Dean asked. Clearly, none of us would be going out tonight—I couldn't anyway. After our ordeal, we just wanted to get home.

Kavi shrugged.

"Sorry. Afraid I have a family thing," Chris said, then widened his eyes. "Oh."

Dean hadn't been asking the rest of us.

Chapter 13

A few days later, I walked Teddy Roosevelt through the Dub-Dub park, savoring his company and my freedom. "Normal" had never felt so good—not since play rehearsal had begun and my life had become subject to outside control.

It was amazing the things we took for granted. With Mr. Pentek's voice in the back of my head, I couldn't help but draw a line to democratic society. Here, we were used to going where we pleased when we wanted to, and pursuing our own goals, not someone else's. At least when the directors put us on their leash, they wanted something positive—I did believe that. Sure, Loretta had some anger-management issues, but the stress of managing a universe full of ... everything might make a guy cranky. Jack probably got more of the equivalent of whatever sex might be in the future, or whatever plane they resided on, hence her more chill demeanor.

Speaking of sex, I had been in a bit of a funk since Friday night when Dean asked Brisa out. Not that I begrudged her that or wanted him for myself. It just sucks to be single, and I had been since before the pandemic. Jeff Polacek had not been much to write home about, anyway. Our freshman romance had lasted all of three and a half weeks—until he had posted to his friends online that I was "plywood," which I'd had to puzzle out from the context clues. These were references to my chest and my mind— flat-chested and dumb as a board, I guessed. Beauty *and* brains, not.

That had really hurt, until B. asked me how much fun I'd had on our two dates and how smart and sexy I thought Jeff was. Suffice it to say, being driven to and from the movies by Mrs. Polacek and discussing how Raisinets looked like rabbit poop had not deeply impressed me. Neither did Jeff's attempt at a "mustache." I might have sniffled over the social post and breakup a bit, but then I went out for fries and Cokes with Brisa and forgot about him. Well, I was nothing if not still available. I could've put up a For Rent sign on my ass.

Ahead at the second duck pond, next to the fake saloon storefront the park had erected near the creek, came a familiar form.

"Hey, Hamad," I greeted Chris, handing him Teddy's leash. He liked to own a dog vicariously through me. Teddy gave a few front-leg skips, happy to see his friend.

The day was semi-cloudy, with the sun jutting through vapor wisps and treetops at irregular intervals. Heading further into spring, the moist air had shocked new growth out of everything, with brighter green outlining every fern, shrub, and tree bough.

"How're your lines going, Carls?" Chris asked. "Want to practice our scene while we walk?"

"Sure."

We were busy running through the old lines and refreshing our memory for Act Three. In it, Tony and Mrs. Hardcastle have a convoluted exchange regarding the golden wrench, which he has swiped and given to Hastings so he can elope with Constance without losing her inheritance. Believing she's been robbed—which she has, but by her own son—Mrs. Hardcastle pitches a hissy fit that Tony exacerbates in truly juvenile manner.

We replayed the scene to that point, and Chris gave his best Tony impression of an asshole, repeating "I'll vouch for that!" over and over ad nauseum. "You do realize, *amigo*, that you've been typecast," I joshed him.

"You do realize," he replied, "that you're old enough to be my mother."

I hit him playfully, no longer upset about having to act my age in that role. But I *was* a year older than Chris, although we were in the same grade at Foster High. He had started high school a year early, being the sort of high achiever that the Hamada family produced. So, I was too old for him, and he was too young for the rest of our crowd, as far as romance went. Or so the prevailing social norm dictated. Then again, he was playing a young man ostensibly courting his first cousin, so how much more of a stretch would a winter-spring romance really be?

He must have read the topic in my mind because he next asked, "Have you heard from Brisa since her date with Dean?"

I could hear a note of envy in his voice, too, even though he likely was not interested in hooking up with either one of them. Like I said, it sucks to be single.

"Sorta. She gave me details without giving me details."

"Sounds about right." He paused to let Teddy explore a favorite bush. "After that night in the woods, I guess I'm not surprised. They're kind of on the same wavelength sometimes."

"I guess I'd be more interested in finding out who Kavi hangs out with," I said. "He's such a mystery."

"I get where he's coming from, though. Reminds me of my family. Parents want the best for us, so they drive us into the ground to 'help' us get there. He probably doesn't have time for women."

"Or men," I suggested.

Chris copied Loretta's voice: "'Don't assume!'" He smiled.

"That's right. You know, it's weird, but I feel like we've actually learned something from our little theater interventions."

Chris cocked his head. "So have Brisa and Dean." He caught my smirk. "No, really. Hasn't made a dent, but they're getting there!"

This made me wonder just how far Jack and Loretta planned to take our education.

***

My answer came in fits and starts, on rehearsal nights for the next three weeks. While the Hardcastles' and their guests' ships passed in the night, the Hot Five got on board every imaginable conveyance to new destinations. We hopped the subway in inner-city New York, the 405 Freeway in Los Angeles, and a tuk-tuk in Bangkok to pursue our earlier "research" into global crime, homelessness, and plastics disposal. When Chris said he thought climate change was the biggest world threat, Jack and Loretta took us by boat to the Mariana Islands and by air—and I do mean, literally, by *air*—to somewhere in Australia. The kangas were a dead giveaway. As exotic as it all was, I was getting desensitized to being airlifted out of my life and dropped into another setting, or act, or scene somewhere else in the world.

What was not, and would never be, normal, though, was *when* they dropped us there. As in, what year it was. And it got hard to tell, right off. Like the suddenly clean riverfront in West Bengal, some landscapes looked contemporary when they might be years in the future. Even judging by vehicle makes and models didn't work. Apparently, car manufacturers found it profitable to copy old fuel-burning model designs in newer alternative-powered vehicles. Although there was that one, short glimpse of New York that the directors gave us, that had *no* vehicles in it. Chillingly, it also had no people.

So, we were absorbing a lot; we just weren't sure how it all exactly applied to anything in our here-now lives. What could we change? How would it change us? Would we even find out? It struck me as highly ironic that this all coincided with my learning to recite lines like, *I tell you, I'm not in jest, booby.*

The others were growing with time as well. Dean had surprised the hell out of us, and Chris especially, by ditching his gas-guzzling Jeep and showing up to a recent play practice in a new black Mustang Mach-E. I guessed those EVs we saw in the there-then impressed him. He was also less quick to blame people who were suffering from adversity for their predicaments; he only asked a group of islanders once why they didn't just move somewhere with higher elevation.

His newfound tolerance was a good influence on Brisa, whose defensiveness was taking much longer to boil over, and whose status as AD seemed to have bolstered her self-esteem, not that her ego needed more stoking. But her bravado had always been an act, meant to set her apart from her elder sisters. This may have opened up some space for Dean to figure out what acting really was. He had gotten pretty consistent in remembering his lines and occasionally imparting some emotion through their delivery.

Kavi hadn't changed so much as come out of his shell, and once he did, there was no shutting him up. Joss had to reprimand him several times to keep quiet at his console, as he started kibitzing with the actors and trampling on her toes. I actually adored this side of him; he was so observant and rational that his advice was usually worth taking. It was easy to think he wasn't a creative type, with his detailed mind, but as he'd told us, in his future line of work, he'd have to think in the outer limits, and he practiced that every now and then.

Chris? I think he was tracking the same path as me, taking what he could from each out-of-body experience and adding it to what he already knew. Whoever thought we'd build a body of knowledge before we hit twenty?

So, as dress rehearsal loomed, I was feeling pretty good about those two settings in my life—the real and the staged. Even when manipulated by Jack and Loretta, I felt as though I'd gained some control over events, or at least my reaction to them. Until it started raining, both literally and metaphorically, and wouldn't stop.

***

"Line!" I called again, somewhere in the middle of Act Four. *Damn it!*

I only had a brief foray onstage in this act, and I could not get my act together tonight.

Brisa read from the script for me: "Take it from 'Dear Tone-Meister, I'm now waiting....'"

Right. Mrs. Hardcastle was reading a note that had come in from Beau Hastings elsewhere on the property, but it was nearly illegible. "Dear Tone-Meister," my distracted rendition of the Missus said, "I'm now waiting for Miss Hardcastle—"

"Miss Neville!" corrected Brisa, starting to sound strained. It was late in the game for these amateur mistakes.

"Miss *Neville,*" I continued, "with a shelf-driving vehicle—"

"*Self*-driving!" Brisa called, exasperated.

Joss waved her arms. "Hold up, hold up! Script, Brisa." She jutted her chin at me. "Just read your lines, Carli, until you get your footing again."

Crap. I could feel Blaze's and Chris's eyes on me as they silently begged me not to blow their concentration too.

I took a deep breath and read, "'...with a self-driving vehicle out in the garage, but I find my Tesla not yet charged and unable to perform the journey. Perhaps you could lend us your old beater to make our getaway, as you promised. And hurry up, as the *hag* (and that's putting it nicely), your mother, will otherwise suspect us! Yours, Hastings.'" I managed to look up toward the seats and feign old-lady fury. "'Grant me patience. I shall run distracted! My rage chokes me.'"

I sighed heavily as Blaze's Constance tried to placate me. Of course, Mrs. Hardcastle was having none of that, coming up with her own "solution" to the elopement. She pretends to be appeased, but then curses Hastings' scheming, vowing to throw a golden wrench into the works—the golden wrench that Spider has found and unwittingly returned to her.

"'I'll defeat all your plots in a moment, Mr. Hastings,'" I threatened. "'As for you, my niece, since you have got a fresh "old beater" gassed up, it would be cruel to waste it. So, instead of running away with your "boo," as you call him, prepare, this very moment, to run off with *me*. Your old auntie will keep you and your plumber's jewels secure.'"

As the two left the stage, Tony was supposed to tell Hastings, who had come looking for him, to meet him in the garage in two hours. Instead, Chris said "garbage," which set off howls of laughter among everyone onstage and Kavi off in the wings. If this was how dress rehearsal was going, I didn't want to predict the success of opening night.

When he finally wrapped the scene, with Tony promising to find the keys to his old car and fulfill his promise to Beau Hastings, a sense of impending doom hung over the cast and stagehands. Joss called a break.

The Hot Five gravitated toward one another, sheepish looks on everyone's faces. One person's screw-up was everyone's screw-up, at this point. Joss had been right: we really were a team. One that wouldn't win a championship anytime soon.

"Don't worry, my friends," Kavi said. "Joss told me that terrible dress rehearsals often precede the best show runs."

"I sure hope you're right," Chris murmured.

"Or else we'll wind up in the *garbage*," I said, digging an elbow into his side and eliciting a watery grin.

Dean was playing with a baseball he'd pulled from the pocket of his jacket that hung off of a folding chair. "It'll all be a piece of cake," he said reassuringly. "Which there will be plenty of ... at the world's greatest *cast party!*"

This did make us feel better, because once we gave three solid performances next weekend, a mighty celebration would be our reward. The Dixons had offered to host the party, and we'd get to see Dean's house for the first time and see his parents as something other than spectators on opening night. My folks would be making a rare appearance together on closing night, and Brisa's and Chris's families had bought tickets for every show. Poor Kavi would have to be adopted by all of us, but he talked to his mother in London every night anyway, so she would almost be there with him.

As folks drifted back from the hallway and bathrooms, I gathered my resolve and tried to calm down. I had practiced and practiced, and had a real feel for Mrs. Hardcastle by now. But more than that, thanks to Joss's ongoing direction, I understood what the audience needed from her, from all of us. Stage actors didn't just speak their parts and use body language, they had to connect with the people watching the spectacle. Our timing and reactions to our counterparts helped us do that. I guessed we'd find out how well it worked next weekend.

Joss reconvened the rehearsal, and Brisa called for places. With only Dean onstage at the opening of the fifth act, the rest of the Hot Five clustered together at the stage-right wing to watch. Just then, I felt something wet hit my wrist.

Then it happened again.

"Did anyone else feel that?" I looked up, but it was dark just outside the range of Kavi's tiny green light.

"Feel what?" Chris asked.

Blip-blip-blip!

"That! It feels like raindrops."

Brisa shushed me. "The pond scene doesn't come up until later," she whispered.

Then a major gush of water hit my head. I jumped out of the stream.

"Ae ma!" cried Kavi. "I believe a pipe has burst!"

The next moment, a torrent poured forth, fritzing out the power to the console. Blueish-white sparks flew, and the green light went out. Everyone started yelling and kind of running in place, not knowing where to turn or what to do.

True to form, just then, the rest of the stage lights dimmed, and once more, my four friends and I were left alone in the black box, silent now but for the sound of running water.

Chapter 14

"**M**y hair!" cried Brisa as she fought her way through a stormy sky.

"My god!" Dean countered, in response to the view from our paratrooper position, some ten thousand feet above sea level and dropping fast. The directors were bringing us in for a closer look.

We lived in a place where it rains pretty consistently for nine months of the year, but I had never seen water like this. We'd been transported to a flood plain of some sort, or a floating city, if Venice were relocated to hell. As we flew in through sheets of rain, I saw what looked like boxcars bobbing in a gigantic pond. But they weren't moving.

What appeared to be short, squat houses surrounded by water turned out to be, on closer inspection, just the top floors or roofs of swamped ones. Little sticks stuck out of the water alongside them, resembling the upright posts of old, forgotten piers whose cross boards had rotted away. They were actually telephone poles—the ones left standing, anyway—and the long, parallel tracks rising out of the drink in random spots, I realized, were portions of freeway overpasses, the rest of the roads sunk, covered over, disappeared.

This land-meets-seascape was mocked by a skyline of tall buildings in the distance where a city center had wisely been built on the highest point in the area. When good decisions are made, though, they don't automatically erase earlier ones. And changing conditions could render the good choices bad. That was something to remember, as Jack and Loretta now pointed out.

"Surprised?" Jack asked. "Wondering how people could build homes so near the water?"

"The city is surrounded by water!" Loretta said impatiently. "That's where the commerce comes from."

"And guess what: the seas are rising," Jack added. "What once was safe may soon be submerged."

Chris struggled to respond in the wind and rain. "So, wait. This is now? Or in the past?"

"You wish," Loretta said.

"It's in the future," Jack informed him.

I had the same next question as Chris. "You're saying that a place that has flooded how many times before just kept rebuilding in the same spot?"

Chris nodded. "That's where the money is," he answered me, confirming Loretta's observation.

"People do not wish to leave their homes. This is where their families are," Kavi put in tenderly, the concern evident in his tone, even as we passed through the residual storm spray.

Dean angled closer to us. "That's how insurance companies operate," he called. "If they give you money to rebuild, you don't get a new location— they stick you back in the old one."

"Even in the future?" I asked the directors.

"That depends," Jack answered.

A crackle of lightning popped none too far away from us, and I screamed.

"Can you change things?" Jack challenged us.

"Yes! Yes!" I yelled. "We'll do anything you want!"

Just then, the hazy, wet atmosphere cleared, and the wind died down.

"Then, tell us, Kavi," Loretta singled him out. "If you could make one change that would help the world solve all its problems, what would it be?"

We glided lower in the sky, switchbacking above the coastal city, zooming toward the skyscrapers at its center and away from the low-lying outer limits. The directors set us down gently in a lovely, old park anchored by massive oak trees and stone bridges that arched over a placid lagoon.

We literally shook off the water we'd just passed through and panted to regain our breath. I watched Kavi take in the scenery as he gathered his thoughts. He wasn't one to mouth off, like Brisa, before he knew what he wanted to say, or to wield the first thing that came to mind, like me, just to be able to respond to a provocative question.

"Nothing is ever so simple," Kavi announced. "This 'change' you are looking for has several parts."

"That's okay," Jack said, intrigued. "Go on."

Kavi ducked his head. "Since you ask." He waited for the rest of us to give him our attention. "Number one: create a single honest source for best information and understanding worldwide, on a real-time basis."

Immediately, Dean called foul. "But who's to say what's—"

Kavi put up a hand. "The truth? This is the trouble. Please let me explain." He removed his eyeglasses and wiped them on the tail of his button-down shirt, which had come untucked in the flight. "One honest distillation of reality compiled from every observable perspective: this is a new form of truth. This is important infocomm—what we used to call 'news.'" He could see more interruptions coming and preempted them. "What it is not, is entertainment infocomm. That is not news, and never should be confused with it. It does us no good in the sustainable governance of civilization. I grant you, Indians and Britons are just as enamored as Americans with entertainment, but there is no reason this desire cannot be fulfilled separately from the acquisition of knowledge."

"Yeah," Brisa said, working her fingers through her damp hair, "that last thing is called school. We already have that."

"No," Kavi corrected her. "That is education, which is much broader in scope and context from the type of objective daily news, or important infocomm, required to help us make choices in our daily lives. And may I point out," he interjected, "that neither of those methods of informing ourselves are inextricably linked with the need to be entertained."

"In fact," Chris put in, "they shouldn't be."

"Yes," Kavi agreed. "This is what I am saying. We must begin from a place of honest transmission of understanding and belief—not to make ourselves 'right,' or to make ourselves money or friends, but just to add to the world's pool of what is the best understanding at the time. This is as close as we can get to truth."

Loretta tacitly approved, saying snidely, "Is it just me, Carli-person, Chris-person, Things 1 and 2—or is this man a much, much deeper thinker than you guys?"

No one answered that rhetorical question, since it appeared that he was.

Jack pressed Kavi, "And this is the one thing that will change the fate of the world?"

"Part one," he said. "Part two is to use the continually improving infocomm to make the best decisions necessary to improve the condition of mankind over time."

Dean threw up his hands and sighed. "Well! Simple! Is that all?" he taunted.

Kavi gave him a knowing grin. *"Simple* is the goal, sir. Not the starting point. Do not confuse *simple* with *simplistic.*"

"Now we're getting somewhere," Loretta said, sounding impressed.

I could practically hear Kavi's engineering gears whirling as he continued. "In every complex system," he said, "selecting the more direct route will be the path toward the best solution."

"Examples?" Chris requested.

"I have many." Kavi moved us over to a picnic table, where we all sat down. "Let us say you have one hundred thousand people," Kavi posed. "How can one extract the best response to a question that is sought and needed in the moment?"

I opened my mouth to opine about elected leadership and representative decision making, but he went on.

"It would seem that a spokesperson chosen by the majority would achieve this. But your democratic system makes it possible to gain power simply by *persuading* more people that one's concepts are sound. They do not actually have to be sound, or superior to those of the opposing political faction."

"There are still honest politicians out there who just want to do their best," Chris argued. "And they bring in teams to support their vision."

"So, here's a question," I said slowly. "How can millions of voters agree on what that proposed vision is? I mean, people interpret things differently. They might vote for someone based on what they think he stands for or what they wish he stands for, and be totally wrong."

"Correct," Kavi said, a twinkle in his eye. "And having just two or maybe three options for leadership still gives us a limited range of ideas, not guaranteeing the best rises to the top."

I felt vindicated.

"In this old design, those whose solutions were not chosen would disagree. In the old way, those who believe they are 'more correct' believe they cannot agree with others who are 'less correct.'" He leaned back on the bench, causing us to lean forward to see where he was going with this. "But disagreement is not the important factor here. The greatest degree of agreement is. What is needed is a larger pool of propositions than can come from two major political parties, or one chamber of Congress, or one president."

Dean was unconvinced. "More people making more decisions with the same prejudices doesn't sound like an improvement to me."

Brisa had a thought. "Is there a way to ID the more—what did you say?—*honest* thinkers? The ones who have less baggage and are more in touch with reality?"

"I believe so," Kavi said. "This would allow each person to decide for themselves whom they trust to interpret events accurately. Basing the world's choices on trust rather than on popular or cosmetic factors would be much more effective."

"Example?" Chris prompted.

"Okay. Suppose we survey those hundred thousand people for their views on, say, whether to build a new school. We first ask what is most important to them on this issue. Is it to make children comfortable? Move them to a better location? Maximize taxpayers' money?" He waited for us to add to the list in our minds.

"Now, let us suppose this issue is resolved to appease some if not all of each priority. The people are happy with this and want to make other big decisions in the same manner. But not everybody has a child in school or has time to weigh all the possibilities and come up with creative solutions. These people can then join with those whose top priorities turned out to be the most salient for the school outcome. It would be a group of like-minded thinkers who could be entrusted to deliver information and options in an honest manner."

"I see what you're saying," Chris murmured slowly. "It's akin to democratic delegation, but it's voluntary and more personal."

"And more goal-oriented," I added. Then a light bulb went on. "It's more about shared agreement than about who is a popular leader, or who has star power, or more money. There are no more winners and losers—instead everyone gets a little bit of what they think is best."

Excitement filled Kavi's eyes. "Correct again."

Jack brought us back to reality. "Tell us, then, Mr. Das, how this meets a global need."

Kavi's chin firmed, and he stubbornly said, "This gives us decisions based on widest agreement and best understanding."

"Instead of fake news!" Dean practically yelled.

Brisa turned a skeptical eye to him. "Then where does that leave the people who are ... what did you say, Kavi? More correct?"

I fixed on Brisa. "This blows 'more correct' out of the water!"

Evenly, Kavi said, "There will be no need for one person to be right when the thoughts of all people are taken into account, assessed for honesty, accuracy, and efficacy, and then distilled to the elements that will serve the greatest good."

Now Chris cocked his head at him. "But who gets to decide what the greatest good is?"

"It is a simple mathematical equation based on all of the collected preferences, taking into account the factual context of the current moment and applied to the hypothetical context of future generations. In other words, while we may each have our own preferences, collective action must satisfy what is best for future humanity."

For a moment, no one said anything.

"Wow," Chris ventured.

"That is nice and neat," I said, uncertainly.

"Out of complexity comes simplicity," Kavi said with satisfaction. "The good kind." He smiled.

"And you'd do this on a global scale?" Brisa clarified. "Every man, woman, and child, here in the U.S., on the Arctic tundra, those people on the Mariana Islands, some guy living in a cave somewhere?"

He nodded.

Dean just blinked at him. "So ... that's not gonna happen," he said definitively.

"But it *could* happen," I insisted.

Before Kavi could join the argument, Jack stepped in. "Well, there's one way to find out."

"What is that?" Kavi asked politely.

Loretta gave an ominous, condescending laugh. "Do it."

***

The wind picked up, and we were no longer seated in the old-fashioned park but now stood on the street in a neighborhood of worn clapboard houses and corner stores. For a city of this size, which we'd gauged from the air on the way in, we saw few passersby. Thunder sounded in the distance, followed by visible shards of lightning. Then it began to rain, and the scattered people around us put up umbrellas and kept walking, everyone bent on getting somewhere.

Even though rain was coming down pretty hard, I mused that carrying umbrellas with metal spokes might not be a good idea in an electrical storm. Then a large gust of wind hit one of them and turned the protective dome inside out. The woman carrying the broken umbrella yelped, dropped it, and ran for cover, just as raindrops the size of baseballs began to batter us.

I reached for Brisa's hand, knowing that her hair might be the least of her worries. She huddled up to me and squeezed my arm instead with both her hands. *"Ay,* Carli! Not again!"

The here-now day back at home had been unseasonably warm, and we were all dressed lightly, in a mix of tee shirts, shorts, light cotton pants, and of course, Kavi's usual long-sleeved Brooks Brothers shirt. Nothing that would keep the rain off, though.

We surveyed the street we were on, and Dean pointed to a boarded-up shop down at the end of the block that had a recessed doorway.

"We can't all fit in there," I said, already out of ideas.

"How is your solution model going to work on this?" Chris asked Kavi, sincerely hoping it might.

Kavi shrugged helplessly, and just then, the front door to the nearest home opened, and a woman came out.

"What're y'all standing here in the wet for?" she scolded. "Are you lost? Storm's coming. You'd best get on inside." She motioned us ahead of her and followed us into the house. It was about as dark in there as it was outside, for marbled clouds had overtaken every bit of sunlight.

The walls rattled as the wind increased, and the sound of rain against the wood siding was louder than I thought water could be. *Wham!* Something solid made contact with the frame of the house, and I fully expected windows to break or a wall to cave in.

"This way!" A man stood at the end of the dim entryway in the rectangle of an open door.

The Hot Five scurried through it, once again shaking off water and heaving from breathlessness. An overhead lamp gave off a weak but welcome glow. Inside were a half dozen more people, standing or sitting on floor cushions and an ancient burgundy-colored sofa whose stuffing spilled out of one hole in the upholstery. They raised their heads in curiosity, not inviting, but not hostile, either.

"I'm Deb," the woman who had greeted us said. "I got food and cold drinks you're welcome to. *Mi casa es su casa* until it's all gone."

I didn't know if she meant the food or the house. Kavi, Chris, Brisa, Dean and I exchanged glances and silently agreed to accept her offer. We tentatively made our way into the room, not knowing what to do next.

Deb went over to a cooler in the corner and started tossing out pop cans, which Dean instinctively caught and handed to the rest of us. The man who had let us in pointed at the others in the room and ticked off: "You got my wife, Deb; and that's Jerrold, Sawndra, and Mack." He pointed to a shadowy corner where an old woman bent over a youngster lying on a sleeping bag. "And there's Miss Lizzie and Cath."

Deb handed him a root beer. "He David." She smiled a crooked and mesmerizing smile.

Lightning seemed to hit just outside and brightened the whole room for an instant. I took it upon myself to introduce my friends and me, but I wasn't sure how to tell them where we'd come from.

"Y'all tourists?" the twenty-something girl on the couch—Sawndra—asked. "You picked the wrong time for a vacation."

The others laughed. The young man sitting next to Sawndra said, "This storm's way beyond what we've seen before. Governor's already ordered the 'vacuation. Didn't you hear?"

That explained the sparsely populated streets we'd seen once the directors put us on dry land. And the direction that so many had been headed.

"What're you doing here, then?" Dean wanted to know.

"Aw, we got no wheels. Cain't get out." He jerked a thumb at the younger guy who stood against the wall holding a trumpet. "Mack said there'd be buses, but there wadn't any."

Mack stuck up for himself. "Tha's just what I heard," he said. "Mr. Friendly down the corner told me that. Now come to find out, him and his family went to hole up down to the football stadium."

"They got 'em a whole Red Cross deal there," Deb explained. "I'd say y'all could go, but it's too late. You'd never make it across town before this bitch makes landfall."

Chris's eyes were wider than I had ever seen them. "And by 'this bitch,' you mean..." he prompted.

"I think they naming it 'Ginny,'" Deb said. "Gonna be Cat Fo.'"

"Cat Five," her husband, David, amended.

Chris's eyeballs just about jumped out of their sockets. "You mean, Category Five, hurricane-force winds?" he peeped.

David nodded. "In the one-sixty, one-eighty range."

Miles per hour? My heart just about stopped. Mom and I got nervous in Worden's Woods if the wind picked up over fifteen. All those towering trees with branches prone to molting...

Kavi's folks had some experience with seasonal winds and rain, and his lowered eyebrows and somber expression told me he'd placed this information in that context. "This wind," he addressed David, "it is accompanied by what volume of rain?"

David swallowed a sip of root beer. *"Beaucoups."*

"And this house, is it near a hillside, or how close is the waterfront?" Kavi was probably calculating the risk for landslides or freak waves.

"Dudn't matter. All that matters is will the levees hold."

Kavi eyed Chris questioningly, who explained to him that levees in the Gulf area were designed to hold back surges of seawater.

"Designed," repeated Jerrold from the couch, "but they gon' fail."

Ever the optimist, Chris said, "I thought the city rebuilt them after Hurricane Katrina."

"Yeah," Jerrold confirmed, "But they goin' on thirty years old now! And the gulf done rose. What they built then ain't ready for what we got now."

The house shuddered as a gale struck its walls.

Brisa scuttled over to me, and we sank to the floor together on a couple of cushions.

Deb flashed us a reassuring look. "We got the Lord, and His light'll see us through."

This hit home with Brisa, but Chris gave me the side-eye. He was a staunch nonbeliever, whose faith rested instead in the power of good intentions and solid effort. I squinted at him as if to say, *Cut them some slack. They need something to hold onto right now.*

So did I. Without Teddy Roosevelt's comforting bulk to give me strength, I reached out one hand for Chris's and one for B.'s.

That's when the lights went out.

Chapter 15

The storm wracked the area all night. With little choice other than to stay put, as wind and rain made a toxic stew, Kavi's decision-making matrix was all but forgotten. We took turns relieving ourselves in a bucket, kitty-corner from Miss Lizzie and Cath's pallet on the floor.

The eleven inmates within the four walls of Deb and David's home filled the endless night with prayer, unspoken pleas, and the occasional pop of soda can tabs and three-note riffs from Mack's trumpet that could be heard during odd lulls. These moments were almost more horrifying than the wind's onslaught, as we wondered whether the next burst would be even greater.

The worst of it came when window glass blew into the other rooms—David had removed the panes in this room and boarded the opening, which did splinter but never gave way completely. But the wind's cries took on a life of their own.

I had never known such sounds—as though the damp air around me generated an unrelenting friction expressed in decibels rather than movement. I could feel the pressure in my chest, between my ears, in the very depths of my soul. Brisa and I hung onto each other for dear life as it all began. Then Deb passed out a couple of blankets to share in the darkness, and Brisa gravitated to Dean's warmth while Kavi snugged up with Chris and me. When, at last, the howling of the wind and snaps of lightning receded to background levels, weak dawn rays signaled a new day that we thought would never come.

In the vacuum of the ensuing silence, I could smell a tide of rainwater outdoors mixed with the odor of all the debris it had carried. But it wasn't unwelcome—far from it. I could literally smell relief.

Relief, I found, is more an absence of an emotion—terror—than a distinct emotion itself. It's a physical sensation, an involuntary unwinding of pythonlike muscles. After a hurricane has passed, relief is also a sound: silence.

We had all largely hunkered where we'd settled earlier, and now we began to rise and move stiffly about to warm ourselves. Brisa and I hugged, and I saw Chris throw an arm around Kavi for a few moments. In their corner, the child named Cath began to cry, and Miss Lizzie calmed her with a litany in her rich patois.

Dean quietly thanked our hosts. "I don't know what we would've done without you."

"Praise Jesus," Deb announced, "we still here."

She and David decided to survey the neighborhood to see which neighbors might need help or if it was safe for anyone to venture out. They took Mack with them.

While they needed answers, the Hot Five had nothing but questions. If this was the future, as the directors had indicated, how far distant? How was it that America hadn't found a way to be ready for disasters, not just react to them? Or, if they had, why were poor people—the ones with no wheels—always left out of the safety net?

Chris asked Sawndra and Jerrold how long ago Katrina had been.

"August 28, 2005," Sawndra recited soberly. "I wadn't born yet, but my grandmomma and most everybody in the parish could tell you all about it. We all know the stories."

In response to another question from Kavi, Jerrold said, "Took the Corps nearly ten years to refit the storm walls, and almost as long for my folks to get back into our damn house. They scrubbed out the black mold, finally got a new roof, and repaired every inch of rotted and busted interior and siding, bit by bit. Then Ida did it in."

Another storm—one that I remembered from the news—a Category Four, David informed us. We murmured in sympathy.

"Making this," Chris whispered under his breath to our group, "definitely *not* now for us."

While our two new friends provided anecdotes of a few more memorable hurricanes in the intervening years, my mind was half a world away—or whatever you'd call time and space travel. People were the same decades down the road? Wearing tee shirts and drinking soda? Climate change had likely pushed this neighborhood closer to danger. If the catastrophic storms were more frequent, why were people still living here? How long could that last? I could see that these people had no means to do much but adapt and survive.

Maybe Kavi's ideas would make a difference. But they hadn't yet, by whenever this was. No way could I ask; these people would think I was nuts. My stomach got that hollowed-out feeling that came from being helpless and hopeless.

Just then, Cath started crying again, and Jerrold asked Miss Lizzie what was wrong.

"I think she just hongry," the woman replied. "Can ya get us something, and some water?"

He produced a half bottle of water and a bag of Macho Nachos from a dwindling pile of snacks. Brisa asked Miss Lizzie if she and the little girl lived here, but it turned out that they were sheltering with Deb and David because their place still hadn't been repaired from the previous hurricane's damage.

"Miss L. take care of Miss C. 'cause her momma died from a overdose," Sawndra explained. "She her grandmomma, but she 'Ma' to all of us in the neighborhood."

"You know I am, baby," Miss Lizzie said.

Touched, Brisa went over and knelt near her, murmuring soothingly to the child and helping her fish some chips out of the bag.

I was struck by the care I was witnessing. In our neck of the woods, people kept to themselves, fussing over their homes and lawns, saying hi in passing on a walk, but pretty much, we were all independent. Apart. Wasn't that how it was supposed to be? The American dream told us we should all be self-sufficient, pulling our hopes and fortunes up by our bootstraps.

I looked over at Dean, who kind of personified that sentiment. But he—Mr. Sports Scholarship and Spring Break in the Alps—was gabbing with Jerrold—a guy looking at minimum wage and no college—as though the two had been litter mates. Meanwhile, Kavi held Sawndra captive with a lively comparison of last night's storm to every monsoon event to ever hit the Bay of Bengal.

After a bit, we heard the front door bang open and hurried footsteps coming our way. Deb, David, and Mack burst into the room and asked for help elsewhere in the house.

Jerrold jumped up. "What's going on?"

"Storm surge. One o' the levees spilled over," David said. "Whole neighborhood's flooding."

Deb started gathering up belongings. "Water rising fast."

"Well, can't we get out?" Chris's voice held a frantic note.

"Uh-uh. It too far to the stadium or even the Navy base. No telling how high this water gonna go. Got to stack furniture, get to the roof."

This sounded like a cartoon remedy. "Is that going to work?" I asked.

"Anything's better'n drowning," Mack replied. He kept his horn in one hand and lent his other one to dragging chairs into a corner, to keep electronics and other things off the floor.

David motioned us into the interior, where we began moving tables and chests beneath an attic hatch in the ceiling. My mind flashed on the watery vista we'd seen yesterday as we flew in. The directors had shown us a preview of where we'd be now. Or was it old footage of the past? It was maddening that the same problems repeated themselves, decade by decade, with nobody in power doing what they could to do things differently.

I wondered again why Loretta and Jack had drawn us into all this. If people arguing over being right or just wanting to make money could keep all of civilization from progressing, what was the future going to look like anyway? How could Kavi's innovations make a dent in this predicament alone, not to mention the rest of the world's struggles?

Then I remembered that eerie scene from our trip to Manhattan—the empty streets, the wind whistling through the landmark buildings. The directors had let us know that what we saw wasn't always what would be, but what might be. Was it possible that the future of the human race might boil down to one really good idea?

***

We managed to build a furniture ladder to get to the attic, which had two windows, now devoid of glass, on opposite sides of the house. David and Mack fashioned a sling out of a blanket and some rope, and Jerrold and Dean pulled Cath and Miss Lizzie up through the hatch in it, one at a time. Cath, though a toddler, appeared to have some disability and couldn't walk, while Miss Lizzie, who might be sixty, seventy, or eighty, was fragile and too unsteady to crawl up the furniture steps.

"Used to be a pull-down stairs through the hatch," Deb explained as she dragged herself through the opening by her forearms. "But that long gone."

We learned the house had been in her family for longer than anyone could remember. That was saying a lot for a wooden structure in a storm and flood zone. Myriad wall patches and mismatched molding showed years of wear, tear, and repair. When Deb's parents died in a road accident and her last sibling moved away, the house became hers.

"Tha's why I married the gal," David joked, squeezing his wife's wrists and helping her over the spray of broken glass on the floor.

They looked too young to be married homeowners, I thought. Hell, they might not be much older than me. Considering I'd had one forlorn romance in my entire life, they were way ahead of me.

Those of us who hadn't gone outside this morning finally had a vantage point from which to survey the storm damage. Where once was order now lay chaos. The mind-bending sight of horizontal downed trees and telephone poles was eclipsed by the carpet of debris—house siding and car tires and bicycles, and bits of unidentifiable things creating a mosaic of crap. Objects that should have been inside garages and cupboards and dresser drawers were now strewn about the ground like lumpy snow. But this layer of personal detritus was on the move. A flow of water down the street caught items and lifted them, washing them up on porches and window sills. That water was rising.

And this was just one street in one neighborhood of the city. *Multiply this reality by thousands,* I thought. Again, the image of what we'd seen from the sky on our way in came to mind. The masses who had escaped by freeway or jammed together in the Red Cross shelter would still have this destruction to return to. Meanwhile, there might be tens of thousands like us, hemmed in by an encroaching sea that had topped the levees and gone looking for natural boundaries.

It didn't find them anytime soon. All day, our hearts rose in our throats along with the water level. The Hot Five stayed glued to the windows. We kept looking for rescue crews or officials of any kind. The locals were less hopeful.

"Police ain't even around," Mack grumbled, still gripping his horn in one hand.

Sawndra waved an arm. "They got out along with everybody else. They wantin' to escape the storm too."

With the power out and Deb's supplies nearly gone, we knew we'd either need the flood to crest so we could get out, or somebody from the outside to ... what? Airlift us supplies to the roof? Fat chance. This wasn't a movie.

"Jesus, B.," I said to my friend. "We might really be stuck here."

Chris heard this and tried to comfort us. "In every other instance, Jack and Loretta took us home before anything truly dire could happen."

Brisa argued, "But that was because Carli or somebody said the right thing or did something to give them what they wanted. I don't see how we can do that now. Even with Kavi on the case."

"Kavi's pretty smart," I agreed, "but he's not magic."

I had a feeling it was up to us this time.

We passed the hours by getting to know the residents better. Fortunately, they didn't ask many questions other than where we were from and where we went to school. When David heard that Kavi was studying engineering, he perked up.

"You going into electrical engineering?" he asked. "Around here, all kinds of support for that. Prob'ly our greatest heroes, though, are the linemen. Every time a storm knocks shit down, Entergy gotta put it back together to get the power back on."

Kavi explained that he was interested in designing transmission systems, so that they could be used to get the electricity from expanding wind and solar generation where it needed to go.

"You come here," Deb urged him. "People gon' love you."

The topic of getting reliable info surrounding storms came up, and Dean started in griping about fake news. "It's one thing to fool people into thinking that space aliens are abducting people via takeout pizza boxes," he said. "But giving out false news during a natural disaster—that's just plain sick."

Chris mentioned, "Our friend here has a really good way to fix that, though."

Kavi again played the guru. "I am working on a new system of news dissemination that will take the guessing out of the game, you see. Where, if I may ask, do you get your weather and news reports now?" he asked.

"My phone has a weather app," Sawndra said. "But it didn't show nothing as bad as all this until late last night."

Jerrold and David used social media for updates, and Mack said he got all his news from his cousin.

Miss Lizzie said she didn't have a phone or a TV, so she had to rely on whoever passed by on the street.

Kavi explained his method for gathering information from all sources and using technology to prioritize and distribute it. "Then," he continued, "these details can be used whenever choices must be made. Anything from what to wear today to how to reduce flooding such as this in the future."

Far from being uninterested or overwhelmed by the concepts, our friends were intrigued.

Mack, who had been tootling on his horn a bit, set it down and said, "If you can pull dat off, you got my vote for gov'nor."

**

By the next afternoon, nothing had been pulled off, up, or down. The water outside had risen halfway up the doors and poured through the downstairs windows, flooding the whole first floor. The only way out was through the attic openings. And it had begun to drizzle again, in tandem with Cath's crying.

"Deb! Y'all!" Miss Lizzie alerted her friends that the girl needed some water, and food as well, but we'd finished all that first thing in the morning. Despair started to fill in the cracks of faith and optimism surrounding us.

At one point, Jerrold spied some cops in small motor boats coming down the flooded street. He hung out the window and yelled at them. "We need some help in here!"

The rest of us clustered around him, reveling in the sight of uniformed officials. But it turned out that they were looking for dead bodies.

"But we needs to get out and get some supplies!" Sawndra begged.

One of the officers just barked, "There is no rescue team at this time."

The other one explained, more softly, "More rain comin'. They'll be along when the weather conditions get better. Gotta land helos safely."

Deb, David, Chris, Kavi, and the rest of us just looked at each other, our hope sliding into our shoes.

But Deb rallied us. "Don't give in to fear. Let the Lord take it from here."

"Amen!" whispered Miss Lizzie from behind her. "Jesus saves."

Brisa repeated the sentiment in Spanish, but she turned to me wild-eyed and pulled me aside. "Carli, I don't know we're gonna make it out of this one." Before I could give her any assurance to the contrary, she went on, "If we don't ... if we die up here, or down in the water..." She choked back sobs. "I want you to know, you're a good friend."

I didn't know what else to say. "You, too, *chica.*"

Now I thought about what my family would think if I didn't return. I wasn't even sure how that would work, since no one knew of our travels. But if they did, would the play cast and crew find out we were missing first? Would anyone ever know for sure what had happened to me? How would Mom and Dad deal with that?

Tears ran down my cheeks, and my nose stuffed up so I had to breathe through my mouth. I wound up practically hyperventilating, big, heaving sobs running up through my chest. Chris, Kavi, and Dean came over and gathered around Brisa and me. All we could do was give each other silent, tense support. We were all in this boat, sink or swim.

The others were still gazing out both windows, searching for any sign of help. Then David said, "Uh-oh. Here come Ray-Ray."

Deb and Sawndra responded with groans.

"Who's Ray-Ray?" Dean asked.

"Trouble," Deb supplied. "He David's sworn enemy. They got into it all the time back when they was both working the auto parts circuit."

"Befo' I found Jesus," David put in, his eyes telling Deb that was enough description. He leaned out the window and called to Ray-Ray. "What you got down there?"

Our group drifted over close enough to see but hung back. A twenty-something guy with box braids and no shirt stuck out of the chest-high water. He was pulling along some kind of a flotation device.

"Found this fish cooler goin' by my house," he said. "Thought if I opened it up, could float out some women and chirren on it, get to high ground."

David flashed a look at Deb. "We got us some up here. Fish cooler, huh? Looks like about a 150-quart deal."

"Floats good," Ray-Ray said. "But it kinda tippy. Could use another bruh to get 'em out one at a time."

Dean moved forward. "I'll do it," he said. "I'm the tallest in the bunch here."

Brisa put a hand out to him. "Don't go. What if we get separated?"

Ray-Ray called back up, "Prob'ly take twenty, twenty-five minutes to get 'em over to a freeway ramp I know.

"You better get started," David said. "We got four women, a old lady, and a kid up here can't walk."

I looked at Kavi and Chris, and Jerrold and Mack. How would they make it out?

"They can come back for us after," David reassured us. He turned back to his rival. "You sure you up to this?"

"Man's got to help his neighbors," Ray-Ray said. "Water's rising, bruh."

Chapter 16

So, that's how it went. We watched as the guys helped lower Dean out the window and into the dark water below using the blanket and rope, like some reverse Rapunzel savior. I couldn't help but think how Dean's feet would stay wet as his Nikes went under first. Grateful, I felt compelled to send him some encouragement.

"Mr. Hardcastle!" I warbled after him. "Take this golden wrench with you for good luck!" I feigned tossing him the jeweled tool.

A grin passed over his intent face as he reflexively caught the air. Then he turned to Ray-Ray, all business, deferring to the local. "I'm Dean. What do we do now?"

The adults had decided that Cath and Miss Lizzie should go first—one couldn't be without the other. Miss Lizzie couldn't have weighed over a hundred pounds, so they were small enough to fit inside the cooler, but would have to somehow stay upright so as not to swamp the thing.

The guys lowered Miss Lizzie down, and Dean and Ray-Ray showed her how to balance on the unstable device. She sat inside and drew her knees up to her chin, with one hand gripping the cooler and Dean holding the other for support. Ray-Ray held her slide-on slippers till she got in, so they wouldn't get wet; then they waited for the child to be lowered down and settle inside.

Cath merely whimpered through the process while the two young men attempted to balance the craft and keep its passengers above the water line.

"Help me, Lord!" we heard Miss Lizzie implore as they slowly moved away from the house.

Deb seconded the plea. "Could be snakes in there," she murmured.

"Please come back, please come back," Brisa said under her breath.

I reached for her hand and didn't let go for a long time.

It seemed as though nothing had looked so wonderful in my entire life as the sight of two familiar forms pushing an empty fish cooler between them when Dean and Ray-Ray returned nearly an hour later. They said that Cath had begun thrashing at one point and the cooler had taken on water, but Dean assumed the lead and hoisted it high enough to keep going. The child and old woman would be cold and wet, though.

Deb sent a blanket along with Brisa, who went for a ride next. Like the rest of the adults, she was too big to fit inside, so the cooler was turned over to use as a boogie board. She'd have to grip the lip of it and let her legs dangle over the side. With her weight spread out, it would float well enough. The two guys had to put the blanket over her and hope it wouldn't soak up too much water.

Before she crawled through the window, Brisa gave me a desperate look but tried to joke. "See you out there, Mrs. Hardcastle. We'll be back in time for opening night!"

"That's right," I said with a weak grin. In my old-lady voice, I called, "And I'm not in jest, booby!"

When it was my turn, the rain had resumed in earnest. I was going to get wet anyway, I told myself, so I tried to put Mom's hypothermia warnings out of my mind. The snakes, however, stayed there, writhing through my subconscious, entwined with the little hope I'd gotten from the progress that had been made over the afternoon. I found it best to leave my thoughts with those back at the house, willing them to follow safely.

Dean grasped one of my forearms, and I clutched at the plastic rim of the cooler, which dipped and swayed with every breath and footstep the two guys took. The water had risen to neck height on them.

"Thanks, Dixon," I whispered. More loudly, I said, "Ray-Ray. I don't know how to thank you for this."

"No need," he said, keeping his back to me as he kept hopping along, pushing off the ground below and bobbing upward, pulling the cooler by its handle through the murky water. "We take care of folk around here. As my daddy used to say, if you cain't make a difference nowhere else, make a difference in yo' neighborhood." He paused to get a better grip on the handle. "Wisht I'd learnt that sooner."

The scenery from my perch was unlike anything I had ever seen in person. Water, trees, cars, and boats where they shouldn't be. Houses left standing like castles within moats. The odd, bedraggled pet paddling or floating by on pieces of debris. And the only sounds came as plaintive cries from other storm victims who needed rescuing. While his energy held out, Ray-Ray promised to send someone for them. But after a while, he had to save his breath, and their pleas just trailed off behind us.

By the time I saw the concrete freeway ramp rising in the distance, I was soaked and really tired from hanging on to the lurching cooler so tightly. When Miss Lizzie, Sawndra, and Brisa saw us approach, they started yelling and waving their arms. "Over here!"

I splooshed off my ride and felt my feet, still in tennis shoes, touch concrete just beneath the water line. While I was grateful for a chance to rest, the two guys turned right back around and headed for Deb's house again. The women helped steady me on my feet; it felt like I'd been at sea for a week. We moved up the ramp to a set of stairs that led even higher toward a pedestrian walkway. The underside of it acted as a roof to keep off the rain.

There I saw a couple dozen cold and wet people in various states of dress, some with shoes, some without. *So, this is what it's like to be a refugee,* I thought. How lucky was I to have a friend nearby?

***

By the time all of our crew had assembled, night had fallen. I couldn't imagine the sensation of making that last trip over in the dead black. At least the rain had slowed.

We could only make out their shapes in the gloom. David slid off the cooler, and Dean and Ray-Ray dragged it up the ramp, puffing with what sounded like the last of their strength, beaching it like a rowboat on concrete sands.

"*¡Gracias por Dios!*" Brisa started crying and fell against Dean's outline. Deb had a similar, yet more subdued, response to her husband's arrival.

Miss Lizzie held Cath at her feet in the blanket. The old woman called out, "Anyone got any food or drink at all? These good boys been he'pin' people all day long."

I noticed she didn't ask for anything for herself or even for Cath.

Somebody nearby offered something, and then, suddenly, a searchlight came on. It was like one of Kavi's stage spots on steroids.

A cry went up from the crowd of people huddled beneath the pedestrian bridge. The light came from a motorboat that bobbed in the deep water a ways away.

The craft wasn't manned by police; someone in our crowd recognized the locals in the boat and hailed them. One of them called, "We got some jugs o' water and some crackers and stuff here. Couple Coleman lanterns you welcome to."

"Jesus Christ," said Chris, standing a few paces from me. "Manna from heaven! It's almost enough to make me a convert."

"Good timing," I agreed, staying where I was. I didn't want to be greedy when others might be more in need.

My friends and I did get a few gulps from the water jugs, and some soggy crackers and a breakfast bar to share. Miss Lizzie gave her portion to Cath, and seeing this, Kavi gave his to Miss Lizzie. We were cold and wet, but we were doing the best we could.

Slightly more comfortable now, I had a look at our immediate surroundings in the glow from two camp lanterns. The concrete abutment reminded me of something.

I dug at Brisa's side with an elbow. "Hey, B. Looks kinda like the place, doesn't it?"

Her eyes widened, and she actually cracked a smile. "Look, Dean. Could be Friday night at home, minus several light-years."

Chris noticed too. "Damn, there's no place like home," he said. "If we ever get back there, guys, I swear I'm gonna kiss the ground."

"The dry ground," I added.

"You do *dat*," Mack said, "an' we'll come take a pitcher."

There was no way to tell him how that wasn't possible.

Someone in the group of strangers asked if anyone had a phone with charge, but nobody did. Someone else asked if anybody had heard news of a rescue operation. That's when the rumors started to fly.

"Not till the power comes back on!"

"Brady say the National Guard bringing them duck tanks, the kind that go on water."

The grapevine had also suggested that police were standing down in order to help looters and make the president look bad.

David spoke out. "Hold up, hold up! We actually talked to some in person. Cops told us no team could get out here till the weather get better," he said, but no one knew whether that meant when the rain stopped or the water receded or both.

I guessed that Dean had recovered some energy, because he started bellyaching about fake news again. "People, people," he called. "If you're not sure about what you're saying, then let us know. Otherwise you might be getting our hopes up for nothing."

Just hearing that made pain flash through my gut.

Then Kavi said, "This is why my new means of spreading honest infocomm will be so valuable."

"What's that?" a man asked.

Kavi proceeded to recap his concepts for compiling honest information, getting the news out to people, and gaining agreement based on the best understanding of that information. Like Chris had at first, somebody wondered who would decide which facts were accurate and how to use them.

"I am still at work on the algorithm," Kavi replied, "but using computer technology that will be made widely available, each person will have the opportunity to access this data. And while it is not practical to use feedback from eight billion or so individuals, I have a solution for this."

"What's that?" an older woman nearby asked, not challenging him but clearly wanting to know.

"As I had mentioned before to my friends," Kavi said, "each person will be surveyed for a broad array of preferences and beliefs, as a baseline for how they think. This data will be run through my algorithms to reveal other like-minded thinkers, and an aggregate will represent them. Then, people will have the opportunity to sign on with an avatar that is closely aligned with their ethos—a way of thinking that they trust to represent them in many spheres of interest."

"Like a proxy?" I said.

"Yes!" Kavi's eyes were alight. He had finally lost his glasses for good, but the lantern glow here revealed that eyes weren't just for seeing but for showing. This idea of his was clearly a passion, a labor of love that he wanted to share with the rest of the world. "I call them avatars."

"Instead of elected officials," David concluded.

Kavi nodded. "Each person selects an avatar to 'speak' and act on their behalf as decisions are made, all based on the best available understanding."

"Otherwise known as facts," Dean translated.

"More like honest beliefs," Kavi amended, "but close enough."

"Well," a forty-something man said, "that takes the politics out of the equation."

"And the money," put in the fellow next to him, sounding impressed.

Jerrold had been quietly taking all this in, and now he said, "There's just one problem, man. If this is all done by computer, and you need a computer to get the news and then give the green light to any action ... what we 'posed to do when the power goes out?"

The crowd murmured in league with him.

Kavi ducked his head, embarrassed. "This, I have not quite worked out yet."

David sidled over and threw an arm around his neck. "Bet you will soon, though." He addressed the others. "Dis man, my friends, is gon' be an electrical engineer."

Now Kavi looked even more embarrassed, but in a good way. "Well, I have a friend who is a coder, and she and I are collaborating to work out the bugs."

"*Bravo, mi amigo,*" Brisa said, pride by association in her voice. "You know I hate bugs."

I gave her a sidelong glance. If B. was making jokes again, I had a feeling we just might survive.

***

We chatted on, getting to know people who had been strangers a few hours before but were now comrades in arms. No one was getting any sleep tonight anyway. Somewhere near dawn, the batteries in the Colemans died down.

As blackness settled around us again, I sensed the atmosphere changing. It felt charged, like all of the downed power lines were coming back on at once. My stomach clutched. Was it another storm coming our way?

Suddenly, I was rising, faster and faster toward the rising sun. *"¡Ojala! Que este mierde se acabó!* B.'s Spanish reaction sailed my way.

I looked around: Brisa, Kavi, Chris, Dean and I were flying once more, high above the sodden city, on a new day. The sight and scope of debris littered beneath us was nearly unbelievable. Cars mired in mud, homes reduced to sticks, tangles of electrical wires all souped up together in several feet of water. I wanted to vomit.

Under some spell, we angled away from the flooded neighborhood toward the tall buildings, as well as a round one I recognized as the football stadium we'd heard about. When we passed it, I could somehow see inside the translucent dome, and I made out a sea of humanity—hundreds upon hundreds of people inside the structure, taking shelter just as we had under the overpass. But here were whole families, couples, singles; old people, young people, infants, with a smattering of belongings at their feet and misery splashed across their faces ... and so many of the faces were brown. They must have been waiting out the storm.

Then we moved on, gaining elevation along with the cityscape, to areas that were less touched or untouched by the destruction. Here, no people were visible on the dry but mud-caked streets or in windows; they had probably gotten out with the evacuation order. *People with wheels,* I thought.

As a gradual creep of sunlight intensified, I noticed my gooshy shoes felt less sodden. My body was set down, and my feet hit solid ground. I wiggled my toes. They were dry!

The light now clearly came from one overhead spot and a tiny green bulb off to my left. The stage.

The Hot Five exchanged glances even as we patted ourselves down, marveling at our dry condition. The expression on everyone else's face must have mirrored mine—one that said we'd just been to Oz and back. We all started talking at once, thrilled to be safe, worried about who we'd left behind.

The puffy sound of a hand on a microphone came over the sound system.

"Well, ladies and germs," Loretta said to us, "I hope this little adventure has shown you that equality is not a moveable feast."

"All of us have a right to know and understand the world around us," Jack said.

"I get that," I said, shuddering at the scenes I'd just seen from the air.

"Ditto," Dean echoed.

"Check it out, Jack!" Loretta said with excitement. "Thing 2 finally put on his big-boy pants."

Jack gave a husky chuckle. "I told you the boy had promise," she chided her companion. She addressed

Dean, "He said you were just a dumb jock who'd been born on third base and thought he'd hit a triple..."

Dean's eyebrows went up.

"...But I said, no, you'd been born on first base and thought you'd got a walk."

"Thanks for sticking up for me," Dean said sarcastically.

"Hey!" Brisa yelled. "What about me?"

"Thing 1," Loretta greeted her. "What's your takeaway from your little trip?"

She cut me a look. "Friends are great. But somebody who's a stranger today could be a friend tomorrow."

Chris cut in. "And a guy who was once your enemy might be the one to save you someday. So, be kind, I guess I'd say."

I thought I'd cry. We felt this sort of ... softness seep into us. I could tell we all felt it. You don't go through something like that together without growing closer, and we were about as close as people could get.

Brisa came over and hugged me. Then she looked up at the speakers in the ceiling. "Wait a minute! You there! We're psyched to be back. But what was it that got us home this time? Who was it that said the right thing?"

Kavi cleared his throat.

"Oh," said Brisa, nodding his way.

"Good work," Loretta said, and not as an insult for a change.

"Well, Hot Five," Jack said, sounding like she was getting ready to go. "I guess we'll see you at the performance. If we're invited, that is."

The performance! My heart leapt into my throat. Then I gave a weak laugh and relaxed. After all that had just happened, I could still get nervous about opening night.

"Tell you what," I said to the directors," we'll save you front-row seats." Then a different worry crept into my mind. We really did not need Joss's play interrupted by another field trip. But I didn't want this one to be our last. I looked out from my mark onstage at the rows of seating that would soon be filled by our adoring fans. "Could you do us a favor, though?" I asked. "Do you think you guys could delay the next flight till *after* the curtain call?"